IN PERFECT HARMONY

When Holly Watson starts work as a PA to music director Ian Travers, she's hoping for a simple part-time job to earn a little extra. She gets more than she bargained for, however — her new boss stirs decidedly unprofessional feelings within her. But she's not the only one so affected: Olivia de Noiret, a beautiful and sophisticated prima donna soprano, also has her eyes on Ian — and makes it very clear to Holly that she's already staked her claim . . .

Books by Wendy Kremer
in the Linford Romance Library:

REAP THE WHIRLWIND
AT THE END OF THE RAINBOW
WHERE BLUEBELLS GROW WILD
WHEN WORDS GET IN THE WAY
COTTAGE IN THE COUNTRY
WAITING FOR A STAR TO FALL
SWINGS AND ROUNDABOUTS
KNAVE OF DIAMONDS
SPADES AND HEARTS
TAKING STEPS
I'LL BE WAITING
HEARTS AND CRAFTS
THE HEART SHALL CHOOSE
THE HOUSE OF RODRIGUEZ
WILD FRANGIPANI
TRUE COLOURS
A SUMMER IN TUSCANY
LOST AND FOUND
TOO GOOD TO BE TRUE
UNEASY ALLIANCE

WENDY KREMER

IN PERFECT HARMONY

Complete and Unabridged

LINFORD
Leicester

First published in Great Britain in 2015

First Linford Edition
published 2016

A catalogue record for this book is available
from the British Library.

ISBN 978–1–4448–3089–7

Published by
F. A. Thorpe (Publishing)
Anstey, Leicestershire

Set by Words & Graphics Ltd.
Anstey, Leicestershire
Printed and bound in Great Britain by
T. J. International Ltd., Padstow, Cornwall

This book is printed on acid-free paper

1

Ian Travers leaned back and studied her thoughtfully for a moment. 'So you know nothing about my work? About what I do?'

Holly met his eyes and settled back into her chair. 'Only what your father told me. That you're a music director, and you need someone to handle your office work on a part-time basis.'

His tone was smooth and there was amusement in his eyes. 'I'm not offering a lavish salary.'

She looked at him and held his glance before she nodded. 'Yes, I know that. Any second job will boost my income. I already have one part-time job: organizing the office at Clarkson's.'

'Clarkson's?'

Holly wasn't surprised the name meant nothing to him. Clarkson's had only opened three years ago. Even though Ian's family had lived in the village for ages, she'd never seen him before, in the shop or anywhere else. Their paths had never crossed when they were growing up. Her parents had moved to the village just before she started at grammar school, and he'd already left it by then. He seldom came home after he went to university; but as soon as he was making enough money as an independent agent, he bought the neighbouring cottage to his parents', and over the course of the last couple of years, he'd spent a lot of money modernizing it. His father told her he still used it as his main address, but he now also owned his flat in London.

She came back to reality. 'It's in Abbey Combe. The biggest one around here.'

He nodded. 'It's a new name to me, but things change all the time. I usually buy my books in London. You think you could manage here? What do you do in the shop?'

Holly straightened her spine. 'Ordering, checking deliveries, bookkeeping, banking, general enquiries. I also handle the online sales and help out in the shop if Bill is short-handed.'

He shifted and played with his pen. 'And you don't mind that — being a jack of all trades?' His first impression confirmed his father's description of Holly Watson. She seemed to be 'a nice, straightforward girl'. It was a pleasant change. He seldom met ordinary people these days. The artists he represented and dealt with were often temperamental and egotistical. The music world was atypical to any other. The people who worked in it were often unusual characters. They needed to be extroverts to perform on stage. Some of them managed that easily; others found it stressful. The prospect of employing someone down-to-earth here in his office was tempting.

Her voice jolted him from his wanderings. Holly smiled and tipped her head to the side. She viewed him with ease and her amber eyes sparkled. 'No; in fact, I enjoy the variety. I love books, and I read a lot myself, so if I help in the shop, unless someone wants specialist information, I can usually cope. Bill is a decent boss, and I like my work.'

Ian leaned forward; there was a flicker of interest in his brilliant dark blue eyes as he viewed her white blouse and noticed the discreet knee-length navy skirt. 'Do you like music?'

'If you expect me to pretend I'm an avid fan of classical music, you'll be disappointed. I like all kinds of music if it's easy on the ear. I like pleasant classical music, and I like pop music too. It depends on the mood I'm in, and who I'm with.' She straightened her shoulders and lifted her chin. Her reddish-brown hair bounced softly around her face. Her fair skin was unblemished; her eyes framed with thick, dark lashes.

The corner of Ian's mouth twitched, and he wondered if he was mad to seriously consider her. 'You do realize that you'll have to deal with well-known names in the world of classical music? I don't expect you to read music or anything like that, but you need to know to whom you are talking on the telephone. Artists often expect their egos to be flattered.'

Holly's gold-brown eyes mirrored her mischievous thoughts. 'Yes, I expect some of them think they are quite fascinating, even if they're not. I imagine I'll be able to pick up names and information from appropriate magazines. I'll create reference cards about any people you represent as I go along. If they phone for information, until I've found my feet, I'll appease them with the promise of a return call. That will give me time to find out who they are, and pass their message on to you if I think it's urgent.' She looked around the small study with its neat modern lines and furniture, but a very cluttered appearance. 'If you don't mind me saying so, I think my first task would be to tidy this office; it looks in a bit of a mess. Your father explained you're always working and trying to catch up when you're here, but it looks like you're fighting a losing battle.'

Ian followed her glance and viewed the haphazard piles of documents, files and indefinable papers and magazines strewn across the furniture and floor. Some of it was covered with a faint layer of dust. Humour flickered in his blue eyes. 'Yes, that would be a good idea. There's an awful lot of information about clients I represent among that lot. In fact, it might help you to familiarize yourself with names if you sort through it all.' He ran his fingers through his thick, ash-blond hair, and it sprung back obediently into place. 'I keep my main files and information about all the people I represent here. Until a while ago, I managed to keep everything up to date, but I'm on the move a great deal, and the number of my clients has increased steadily.

Finding something among this chaos gets more difficult with every passing week. I often need to refer to a previous contract, expense account, conditions, etcetera.'

Holly's eyes twinkled, and she replied philosophically, 'I see. Your father did mention that you spend a lot of your time swearing when you're here.'

Another flash of humour crossed his features. He gestured to the piles. 'Only because I get so frustrated. I waste more much time looking for things than actually working, these days. It's a never-ending vicious circle. And the piles get bigger every time I come home.'

She gave him an encouraging smile and nodded. 'It'll clearly be one of my main tasks for a while, but we'll get there in the end.'

Suddenly, he found himself trying to explain. 'When I started organizing concerts and musical festivals years ago, I was usually on the spot for a while and I had a team to help me, paid by

7

the festival committee. Now I'm on the opposite side of the fence, I'm trying to arrange appearances for my clients. I spend a lot of time in London, but I also travel a lot, because the work is so international these days, and being on the spot often tips the balance when I'm trying to persuade someone.'

Holly nodded and waited.

Talking to her reminded Ian how much had changed in his life in the last couple of years. These days, he lived in a world where flattery, false adages, and clichés were run-of-the-mill. He hoped it hadn't rubbed off on him too much. It was his job to negotiate the fees for appearances for his singers and musicians. He earned a set percentage on every deal he clinched, and it was an interesting life. This girl belonged to another world, far different from the one populated by artists and musicians. The idea of having someone like her handling some of his day-to-day business was tempting. He looked at her and decided there was something about her that wakened his interest and his trust.

'It's strange we've never met before, isn't it? After all, we come from the same small village.'

Holly shrugged. 'My family only moved here just before you went away to university. You didn't spend much time here after that, and you're not around much even when you come down on the weekends these days, are you? I can't remember seeing you before either.'

'Dad says you live on the other side of the village.'

'Yes, in Railway Terrace. It curves down to the playing field.' Holly paused. 'I hope you don't think I'm being pushy? Your father suggested I ask.'

With a glint of humour, he said, 'He suggested it to me too. He's probably fed up with me acting like a headless chicken when I'm here.' His expression sobered. 'To be honest, I've never thought about employing anyone, but the prospect of offloading some work is tempting. If you need extra work, it'll suit you too.'

Holly was acutely aware of his lean physique and his good looks. She nodded. 'I've known your dad ever since my parents moved to the village. He's a nice person. I like him.'

Ian studied her more carefully. She wasn't a raving beauty, but she was young, and very attractive. She had regular features, and her amber eyes, flecked with gold, were quite arresting. His knowledgeable eyes noticed her clothes were off-the-peg, classic in style. If she had a limited budget, she wouldn't be able to afford the kind of extravagant fashions he faced constantly these days. Her shiny hair formed a soft frame around her face, and her nails were neat and pale pink. She also seemed to be intelligent and polite. Somehow, he knew she'd be able to handle his clients. Her experience in handling customers in the shop would help her there.

Holly explained, 'I always hoped the job in the bookshop would turn into full-time employment, but Bill is already struggling. He's fighting chain stores and Internet sales. If I don't find something to supplement my income soon, I'll be forced to move away. I'd like to find my own flat locally, but I need a steady job first. I live at home at present.'

'Have you always lived at home? That's unusual in this day and age. Most girls of your age can't wait to leave to enjoy their freedom to the full.'

'I presume you mean the freedom of living with a boyfriend? It may sound old-fashioned, but that's not what I want.'

Ian couldn't help asking, 'Isn't it difficult when you have a boyfriend? You'll want to be on you own with him sometimes.'

Holly shrugged. 'If a boyfriend thinks having somewhere to be alone is more important than gradually finding out if you really like each other, he isn't worth bothering about.'

Ian listened and mused. She was certainly different. The majority of young people these days lived in a haze of 'what the hell' and one-night stands. The fact that his father knew her and liked her spoke in her favour. She'd probably talked to him more often than Ian had himself in the last couple of months. He always seemed to be on flying visits whenever he came home.

His father had still been working when Ian's mum had died three years ago. At the time, Ian had thought that his father's job, plus looking after himself and the cottage, would fill the gap and keep the bereaved widower occupied. It had, to some extent — but then came early retirement, and now his father had more time on his hands. He must feel lonely sometimes.

They'd never talked much about how he was coping, or how he missed Mum. Ian had a bad conscience about that. The right moment to talk never seemed to occur, and he was always on the run . . .

He pulled himself together and concentrated on the task in hand.

Holly remarked, 'This is your main business address. Why don't you use the one in London? That would impress people more, wouldn't it?'

'I don't think so. People in the trade know me by now, and these days I don't spend more time in London than I do here. I honestly like the idea of you keeping things under control here, and having a central address where people can contact me all the time. You do realize it's only for a couple of hours a day?'

'That would suit me fine. Together, the two jobs would be perfect, especially if you don't mind me coming in the afternoons.'

For someone who'd spent his working life in the straightforward, well-organized framework of the world of music, the idea of a handling a job in a country bookshop in the morning, and then the office of a musical director for the second part of the day, was difficult for him to imagine. He hesitated but only for a moment. The paperwork was multiplying quicker than he could ever sort it out. He'd almost missed out on an engagement for Sun Hai Long in San Francisco last month, because he'd mislaid the contract and couldn't remember where he'd put it. It had annoyed Hai Long, and thrown shadows on Ian's ability to handle negotiations. Keeping up with the details of administration was getting harder, and finding previous documents among the growing chaos here in the office was a disheartening and time-wasting process. His reputation had grown steadily in the last couple of years, and the workload with it. He dreaded to think what his tax advisor would say if he had to hand over the details of his income and expenses at the moment. Nothing was in an acceptable form.

'You can cope on your own? I don't

have time to sort out tax, health insurance, or anything like that. And I don't have a lot of time to explain much, either.'

'Unless you have a very unusual system and want me to religiously stick to that, I'm sure I can manage on my own. I'll organize it along the usual lines. If I need to be extra-careful about something in particular, just say so. I don't envisage too many problems. I'll pick up details of your clients and whom you've engaged in the last couple of years as I go along.'

He swept his hand around the room. 'It's all there, or in the filing cabinets. I can send you an up-to-date list of the artists I represent at the moment via email. The details about when they appeared, and where, is among that lot — or filed away.' He nodded towards some metal filing cabinets along one of the walls. 'The folders in the files over there are fairly up-to-date — well, they were up until the end of last year.'

'That means a lot of old clients will

already have a folder in the cabinet. Any new additions will join them as I go along. Eventually, you should be able to find everything filed in its proper place. When do you intend coming down again, any idea?'

Ian was pleased she'd already begun to think about how to handle her tasks. 'As a matter of fact, next weekend, if everything goes to plan. I don't always manage a regular visit. Most of my important clients already have my phone number or email address, but some will try to contact me here for some reason.'

'How have you kept contact with someone who tried to reach you here, if you're away so much?'

'Via email, texts, messages on the answering machine . . . and my father even took messages if he happened to hear the telephone and got to it in time. I prefer text messages whenever possible; it's annoying to be disturbed if someone only wants to ask you about something that could wait. A silent text is not only efficient, it's also controllable. You're familiar with computers and modern technology?'

'Of course. No office can function without them these days.'

He nodded, relieved that she wasn't bothered by the prospect of being left to her own devices. He met her eyes and considered briefly again, before he finally said, 'Well, shall we give it a try? If you think you can manage, it'll suit me. It gives you an extra income, and it probably relieves my father of some hassle too.'

A wide smile decorated her face and the corners of her generous pink lips turned upwards. 'Yes, gladly.' She struck when the iron was still hot: 'When would you like me to start?'

'You can choose. How about the beginning of next week? What about three or four hours a day? Most artists are more active in the second half of the day, but that depends on where they are in the world at that moment, of course.'

'That's fine with me!' She searched

through her bag for her wallet and took out a visiting card. Handing it across the desk, she said, 'That's my home address and telephone number. If something crops up and you can't contact me via my mobile, my mother will take a message, even if I'm not at home.'

He took the card and looked at it briefly, then searched in the drawer for one of his own. 'And there's mine.' He stood up and held out his hand. Holly got up, shook his hand, and looked at him. 'Here's hoping it'll be of mutual benefit for us both. Do you want to call in again before I leave, in case you think of something else to ask?'

She shook her head. 'No, I'll try to manage on my own. It'll be a waste of time for you to go into details of how things work. Next time you come in, give it the once-over, and then you'll be able to judge if I'm coping or if you want to make adjustments.'

Holly was pleased. Even if it didn't turn out to be long-term employment, it meant more money, and gave her more leeway to look for something full-time. Once she'd organized his office, Ian Travers might throw her out again, but she had to take that chance. Her hand was lost in the warmth of his grasp, and she smiled at him again automatically.

He said, 'Yes, okay. I'll give my father a spare key before I leave, then you can come and go as you like. You're welcome to use the kitchen downstairs for coffee, etcetera. Oh . . . and Millie comes in once a week to clean through for me.'

Both their hands fell to their sides, and Holly hoisted her shoulder bag to a secure position before she gave a slight nod and turned towards the door. He made a move to accompany her, but she lifted her hand.

'Please, don't bother . . . I know my way out!'

Ian didn't protest. He stuck his hands in the pockets of his soft corduroys, watched her leave, and listened to the patter of her heels on the wooden stairs. A minute or two later, he heard the front door closing, and stood lost in thought at the window. He saw her walking past the garden of the adjoining cottage where his father was busy tying a bunch of tall golden flowers to supports. Holly gave him a wide smile, and his father's tanned face nodded back. They chatted for a moment, and then Holly went off down the lane. Ian felt a stupid twitch of envy as he noticed that his father and this girl were already firm friends. He turned away. He calculated quickly what she'd cost him annually. Somehow, he already knew it'd be money well spent.

2

His dad told Holly that Ian didn't come home every weekend. She didn't mind. She didn't need someone staring over her shoulder all the time. Ian seemed to be a pleasant person, but she preferred time on her own to sort out the office muddle.

Once she started, she soon discovered that he'd had an efficient filing system at one time, but it had spun out of control. She attacked the dustiest pile first, checking for important papers, or any information about names on his list. If she found anything appropriate, she filed it or made a new folder for that client. She also copied the names and the professions onto a rotary card file of her own as she went along, hoping it'd help her when someone phoned. No one did for a couple of days, then two did in quick succession. She passed their questions on to Ian by text, and he acknowledged them and said he'd sort it out.

When she was working, she often found herself thinking about her new boss. He was an attractive man, in a craggy sort of way. His chin was square, indicating his determination and willpower. His lips were generous, and he had white teeth and arresting blue eyes. From the way he'd organized his office in the past, she guessed he was a logical person. His hair was blondish, short and tapered neatly to the collar of his shirt. He was well-built with wide shoulders and narrow hips, and he wore expensive clothes. In comparison, her other boss Bill looked like a hobo. Holly imagined that Ian's looks also impressed his female clients.

She sighed, and added another name to her rotary card file from the glossy pages of a concert programme. If she ever found a matching picture, she glued that to the card, too. It was nicer to have a physical image of someone among the information if they ever phoned.

Holly bit on the end of her pencil. Yesterday a violinist had phoned who wanted something in his contract explained. His name wasn't in the files. She'd sent Ian a text, and he'd replied that he'd sort it out. She hoped he didn't mind her passing on queries she couldn't solve herself. She aimed at eventually saving him as many calls and enquiries as possible.

A couple of days later, she was surprised when she came into the office on Friday afternoon and found him there. For a moment she was flustered, and she coloured. How silly! Where was her poise? In fact, she felt more nervous today than she had when he'd interviewed her.

'Oh! Hello, Mr Travers. I didn't realize you were coming today.'

Ian liked her quiet oval face, with its dark arched eyebrows and small nose with a slight tip at the end. Her figure was good and slim. She barely reached his shoulder, but she stood straight and had a good posture.

He had noticed a difference as soon as he entered the office. Some piles of papers and magazines from one of the corners had disappeared, and the desk was clear. It looked like she was efficient and didn't need constant instruction or supervision. If she continued like this, his life would be a lot easier.

'I flew in from New York this morning and came straight here.' He gestured around. 'It looks a little tidier already.'

'I didn't know if you wanted to check what I've rejected. Do you? I can keep everything and put it in boxes in the cupboard, if you like. If you don't, I'll put it out for the paper collection.'

He ran his hand through his hair. 'If you've picked out the important bits, I don't honestly think I'll ever have time to go through them later. Any contracts or official-looking papers are vital, though. Keep them! Sometimes I have to refer back to them. You can get rid of the rest if you've picked out the relevant parts. Did anyone call?'

'Only one person; he rang Wednesday. He wanted to know something about his contract. I told him to send you a text.'

'Oh, yes. Frank Quint, right? He sent me a message. Any problems? Any questions?'

She shook her head. 'Your system is easy to follow, and I'm beginning to sort out the backlog. I'm also entering anything relevant into your ledgers as I go along, but I haven't found very much so far. If you have any travel expenses, hotel bills, that kind of thing, bring them with you next time so that I can enter them in the ledgers. You haven't asked me to do any typing either, but it is quite easy to send a document via the Internet. You could then print it out at your end.'

His expression lightened. 'I've piles

of expenses in my top drawer! I'll bring them next time for you to enter them. I hadn't thought about you typing for me, but it's not a bad idea. You could use previous letters or contracts as a pattern, and I'd only need to fill in the details. Up until now, I've wasted a lot of time typing with two fingers.'

'I'll be glad to have other things to do once I've cleared the all the backlog.'

Ian began to realize that this was an excellent idea. For the first time in months, he looked forward to a fairly relaxing weekend. He checked the time. 'I think I'll persuade Dad to go down the pub with me for a meal later on. I have to leave again early tomorrow to catch a flight to Tokyo.'

Holly picked up her notebook and pencil. 'He'll enjoy that. He's very proud of you, and I think he misses you a lot.' There was a hint of censure in her voice.

Ian stuck his hands in his pocket and viewed her with irritation. This woman knew nothing about the kind of life he led, and how difficult it was to fit personal wishes into his schedule. Despite that, he felt slightly annoyed with himself a moment later, because he found he was justifying himself. 'I haven't had any spare time for pub visits for a while, as you can judge by the state of this office. We get on, regardless of that.'

Holly nodded. 'He knows that you are very busy. He never complains, although I was worried about him for a while.'

Slightly surprised, he asked, 'You were? Why, in particular?'

'Oh, he's a lot better now, but at one time I did wonder if he'd end up with depression. My gran slipped into a black hole after my granddad died. It took a while to pull her out of that. In the end, we found that she needed new activities to fill her time. After your mother died, your dad crept into his shell for quite a time, too — especially after he retired. I noticed he was often down in the dumps whenever we met, so I thought the same idea might be the solution for him too. I persuaded him to join the darts team, and the historical society; and my dad collects him to go down the pub for a pint some evenings. He now has interests that get him out of the house and together with other people, and that's made a big difference. I love listening to him playing the piano. I can hear him up here when I'm working. It's clear where your interest in classical music comes from. He's even taken me to a couple of concerts, and organized trips for other people. He's thinking about founding a music society in the village. That'll be good — not just for him, but for others, too. They intend to have talks and discussions about composers, and organize visits to concerts and music festivals and the like.'

It took all of Ian's willpower to keep his mouth shut. This was all news to him. He knew that his dad was an enthusiastic gardener. He kept his own and Ian's gardens in perfect shape. The other pursuits Holly mentioned had caught him by surprise, and his conscience started to prick him again. He should have spent more time finding out how Dad was filling his time. Holly knew more about his father's present interests than he did. His brows straightened.

Holly wondered why he looked stern. She picked up another bunch of papers and started to spread them out.

Ian Travers was rattled: he didn't like the idea that other people were more concerned about Dad than he was himself. He turned towards the door. 'I'll leave you to it. I have a couple of things to check, but they're in my briefcase. I'll do that in the sitting room. I'll probably see you next time I come home — unless I see you down the pub this evening?'

'No, not tonight. I'm going to the pictures with a friend of mine later on. The latest James Bond.'

Trying to keep the irritation out of his voice, Ian said, 'Enjoy yourself, then.' Sounding much calmer, he added, 'And please call me Ian. 'Mr Travers' sounds abominably formal.' Her open, friendly attitude had scored with his father, and he could understand why. Holly gave him a generous smile, and for a moment Ian studied her intensely.

'Fine by me. I'm Holly; but you know that already, don't you? If you're not downstairs when I leave, I'll see you next time round.'

* * *

It took a couple of weeks to get the office into fairly decent order. It was a slow process of checking and listing, but it paid off. Gradually, some phone calls came through from someone Holly had on her rotary card file, and she was pleased to be able to hold a halfway-intelligent conversation with them, even if she could only sometimes suggest they contact Ian for a decision about something.

She was only a go-between, and they knew it. She could only tell them he was away on business, and offer his email address or mobile number. Anybody who expected her to solve his problem was disappointed. That wasn't her job. She only passed their messages on if people asked her to, and he then either contacted them himself, or sent her a text with the appropriate answer. He did phone her briefly from time to time, mostly for information from one of the files. Gradually, they adjusted to each other, and worked hand-in-hand.

⋆　⋆　⋆

When she heard Ian wasn't coming home on the weekend, she felt a bit disappointed. It was a silly reaction, because she wouldn't have seen him anyway, and he wasn't her type at all. He was too busy and too serious. She was tempted to label him as stiff and conservative. Even their phone calls were very business-like and there was no chit-chat. Despite that, she knew there was a friendlier character under the outer shell. She mused that perhaps someone who spent most of his life talking to people about business might fall out of the habit of holding normal conversations. She felt needlessly pleased when she came to the office one Monday afternoon and found a hastily-written note on her desk.

Hi Holly,

It's beginning to look good. I was home on a flying visit and I actually found the information I needed without searching for it for hours. Once you've everything filed, I suggest you check all the files in the filing cabinet again. I have no doubt that in the past I may have put things in the wrong folder in my haste. It's a real luxury to find the information I need without a hassle. Keep up the good work!

Ian.

Holly read it through a second time and decided that, even if he seemed conservative, anyone who said 'thank you' to an employee, in any kind of form, did have the right attitude. It gave her the encouragement she needed to carry on.

That afternoon, during the course of further tidying, she also came across a newspaper article that was a few months old. It showed a picture of Ian escorting Olivia de Noiret, a world-renowned soprano. She was an exotic-looking, beautiful brunette. From the contents of the accompanying article, it looked like she might be Ian's current girlfriend, because they'd been seen together on several occasions. The press was certain they were more than mere professional colleagues.

Holly felt a twinge of regret, because somehow she'd been hoping that her new boss was unattached; although she didn't understand why she should care. She studied the picture closely, and agreed with the reporter that they were an attractive pair. He looked very handsome in evening dress, and Olivia's figure left nothing to be desired. There was something about a tuxedo that added to every man's appearance. On a man like Ian who was already attractive, the result was even more impressive. Holly doubted if Olivia was interested in him for purely professional reasons. A prima donna didn't need to crawl to any agent to get the right parts on the world's opera stages.

Holly studied the photo, and mused that the days when sopranos had figures resembling barrels was well and truly a thing of the past. Olivia could have been a leading lady in any movie. She was rich as well as very talented. Her dress clung to her figure in all the right places, and her jewellery wasn't paste, either.

Holly laid the cutting aside and got on with some serious work.

★ ★ ★

She never worked in the bookshop on the weekend, although Bill sometimes did ask her to come in for a couple of hours if he anticipated it would be busy, or if he needed help for some other reason. Working for Ian on the weekend wasn't part of the arrangement, and it wasn't necessary.

★　★　★

Holly usually had a cup of coffee and a short break halfway through her after-noon job in Ian's office. Harry Travers soon cottoned on to that, and came to join her. She knew that he enjoyed a chat, and she encouraged him to share a couple of minutes with her.

Harry made himself comfortable and poured them some tea. Holly smiled and picked up the newspaper cutting. 'Look what I found.'

Harry took a sip, and then reached forward to look at the article. 'Oh, yes. I remember that. I cut it out of the paper at the time for him. I decided to ask Ian about her, because he'd never mentioned her, and I wanted to know if there was a chance that a world-famous soprano would end up as my daughter-in-law.'

'And?'

He shrugged. 'Ian was as evasive as ever, but he didn't deny they were friends, so I thought there might be something behind the rumours.'

Holly stirred her tea and cradled the mug in her hands. 'That article is weeks old.'

He shrugged. 'Who knows? He meets lots of women in the course of his job. Olivia de Noiret is just one of them. Perhaps it was just business.'

She shook her head. 'From the way they're dressed, it looks more personal than that. The press thought it was worth a mention. Have you ever met her?'

Harry chuckled. 'No. Ian has rarely brought anyone home. From her appearance, I can't imagine Miss Noiret fitting into rustic surroundings.'

Biting a corner off one of the biscuits and shoving a crumb back into the corner of her mouth with the tip of a finger, Holly said, 'Why not? Perhaps somewhere like this village is just what you long for when you spend your life living in the limelight.'

'It's hard to imagine Ian getting attached to any woman after what happened between him and Juliette.'

Her curiosity was enormous. Holly asked, 'Juliette?'

'Oh, you probably don't remember. Ian was engaged to Juliette Keller.'

'Really? I recognize that name, even without my card file. She's a cellist, isn't she? I haven't heard much about her for a long time.'

'Yes! A very nice girl, and a very talented cellist.'

Holly's brows lifted, and she felt disappointed for a few seconds, until Harry continued to satisfy her interest. 'She was a brilliant musician, until she started touring around with a modern pop group. It was intended as a PR booster in the beginning, although Ian tried to talk her out of it from the very start. He warned her it would have a negative effect on her classical career. He was right. She got involved with the lead singer. She earned a lot of money fast, but her talent suffered in the process, and it ultimately ruined her reputation. One thing led to another, and she broke off their engagement because she got hooked on David Allydyce instead of Ian. Have you ever heard of him?'

Holly sipped from her mug. 'Allydyce? He's the lead singer with that Irish group, isn't he? Yes, I've heard of him. He's often mixed up in scandalous behaviour. His name is in the papers regularly. The police have arrested him several times.'

Harry nodded. 'Yes, he's always been a huge name in the pop world, and has managed to stay on top despite all the bad publicity. He fascinated Juliette from the start because he was so different to anyone else she'd ever met.

He seemed to like her, too, in his strange way. Ian put up with the headlines and insinuations for a while, and then set her an ultimatum: it was either him or Allydyce. She opted for Allydyce.'

He sighed. 'I can remember how quiet and shy she was when Ian brought her home for the first time. She was about nineteen. My Anne was alive then, of course, and we were so happy about the prospect of Juliette joining our family. Anne was shocked when they broke up, and she never understood why she ousted him.'

'I bet it upset Ian, too. From what I know of him, I don't think he'd take something like that lightly.'

'No, it changed him. He was always a serious-minded person by nature, but in those days his character was also tempered with fun, and plenty of enjoyment too ... until all that happened. He was a lot younger too, of course, and that makes a big difference. Juliette's decision floored him for quite a while. Ian's humour does come through now and then these days, but I wish I could see it more often. No one can change the past, of course, but I wish I could blot out the whole episode. He would have been better off if he'd never met Juliette.'

'Perhaps Olivia de Noiret will fill that gap.'

He shook his head. 'Not according to what I've read about her. If you'd ever seen her being interviewed, and if you look at her photos more closely, you'll see that there's a hard edge to her. Undoubtedly she's a brilliant soprano but her climb to professional fame has toughened her as a person. I hope that Ian doesn't make another mistake. Juliette was probably too immature, and I think Olivia de Noiret is the opposite. I still feel furious with David Allydyce for enticing Juliette away.'

Holly put her mug back on the tray. 'Surely it's better that it ended like it did? She couldn't have loved Ian otherwise she wouldn't have chosen Allydyce. Perhaps she was immature, or just didn't know what love was until she fell for Allydyce. If she and Ian had stayed together, they might have ended up getting a divorce later on, anyway. Juliette might have easily met someone else later who attracted her more.'

'You're probably right; but it hurts when you see your children are sad, no matter what the reason is. It happened years ago, and Ian never mentions her. My wife used to talk to him about what happened, whereas I never wanted to rub salt in the wound. Although, I do think he's over her now.'

'I expect so. Ian is mature. He knows his way around the world. You have to respect his decisions and way of life, no matter how much you might like to interfere.'

'Oh, I would never interfere. I know he's not stupid, and he's not gullible any more, either. It was a hard lesson for him to learn.' Harry got up and took the tray. 'It's just difficult for any parent to stand back and keep their mouth shut!'

She laughed. 'Harry, he's not a child anymore. Don't worry. I'm sure he knows what he's doing.'

'Hope so.' He gave her a smile and looked at the papers spread out on the desk. 'I think I ought to leave you to it.'

'Yes, I am being paid to work. Are you coming down the pub tonight?'

'I haven't decided.'

'Oh, come on. There's a darts match against Little Coombe. We need some extra players. They even want *me* on the team because they can't find anyone else! My aim is so bad that everyone moves at least three yards away from the board when it's my turn to throw. I notice that, and it's not very flattering!'

Harry laughed. 'Yes, I noticed too; but it's not without reason. You were pretty hopeless, I told your dad, last time you played. They also shut the pub's cat out the back when they hear you're on the team!'

She pretended to look offended.

'Well, we can't all be champions. Do come, Harry! Dad will be there, and Percy Wilson too. I'm their last hope if they can't find anyone else.'

He grinned and nodded. 'Okay. I'll come for the cat's sake. What time?'

'Eight o'clock. Shall I call for you?'

'No, I'll see you there. I just hope there's nothing good on the TV tonight, or I'll have to wrestle with the controls of my damned video recorder again. I'll never understand how it works. Every time I use it, it seems to need different commands.'

She went with him to close the door. 'Then you're doing something wrong. When you get it right, write it down straight away, and then you won't have to think about how to do it anymore. Or perhaps you ought to get a recorder that isn't so complicated.'

3

The following Thursday afternoon, the phone rang.

'Good afternoon! Ian Travers' office. Can I help you?'

'I'm hoping you can do just that. Hello, Holly.'

She jumped at the sound of his voice, and didn't understand why she felt flustered every time she heard his voice. 'Ian! Hello! What's the problem?'

'To cut a long story short, I need a contract, and I need it fast; by tomorrow afternoon at the latest. I hope it's already filed and you can find it easily.'

Her heartbeat had returned to normal, and she also sounded quite sensible. 'A contract? For whom?'

'Daniello Pagnina, I think it was back last June for the Edinburgh Festival.'

'I'll look for it straight away.' She

looked at her wristwatch. 'But there's not much chance of it reaching you by post tomorrow now. The last collection has gone. I could send it by special courier, but I'll need to find one first, and I wonder if I can sort that out fast enough for certain delivery tomorrow morning.'

There was a pause. 'Is there any chance of you bringing it personally? If you could, I'm certain to get it on time.'

Her mouth was dry. 'Can't I just read what's in it to you, or fax you a copy?'

'Unfortunately, there's a heated contention between him and the organising committee of an event where he's supposed to appear. To be honest, I think he's trying to swing the lead. Apparently he's kicking up a hell of a fuss about not being treated like he thinks he deserves. He presumes free hotel accommodation for him, his wife, and a personal interpreter, etcetera, was all part of the contract. I can't remember if there were any special clauses about that, but normally contracts only cover the actual performance and his accommodation. Anyone else he brings, or employs, is his business. I need the original contract just in case there's an ensuing legal wrangle.'

Holly nodded unseeingly at the phone and thought about the next day. 'I can ask Bill for a couple of hours off tomorrow morning, but I can't guarantee he'll agree. It's very short notice.'

'I realize it's a nuisance for everyone; but it is very important, Holly, otherwise I wouldn't ask. If you give me Bill's number, I'll talk to him and explain.'

She paused. 'No. Leave it to me. He'll know I wouldn't ask unless it was necessary.'

'If you catch the eleven o'clock train, or even a later one, you'll get here in plenty of time. I've managed to postpone the meeting with these people until 6 p.m.'

Holly's mind was still catching up.

'I'll look for it straight away, then I'll clear things with Bill. If he has no objections, I'll send you a text confirming.'

He sounded relieved. 'Good. When you get to London, take a taxi to Flat 2A, 24 Bourne Avenue, W2. You'll be my lifesaver. If I had time, I'd drive down and fetch it myself, but I'm stuck here this evening with the director of a musical festival that's being planned in Canterbury in November. I also have a breakfast appointment with someone from the Albert Hall first thing tomorrow morning, and he won't be happy if I put him off at the last minute. That's why I might not be even able to meet your train.'

'No problem. If you're not at your flat when I arrive, I'll just wait there until you turn up.'

'Do that. You can go straight up to the flat. There's a concierge, and I'll tell him to let you in.' He paused. 'Is Dad okay?'

'Yes, I think so. I haven't seen him

today; he's gone fishing with someone.'

His surprise was audible. 'Fishing? He's never done that before!'

'I'm not sure how interested he really is. I think he likes going along with Peter just for company. You need a licence to fish, don't you? He seems to enjoy it; otherwise he wouldn't go. It's not my idea of fun, sitting on a river bank keeping quiet for hours on end.'

'Oh, it has its attractions, once you get used to it. A friend and I used to fish in the local river when we were youngsters. We definitely didn't have licences. We didn't even think about such things in those days. Let me know once you've sorted things out.'

'If the contract is here, I'll find it.'

* * *

Holly looked around Ian's flat. It was modern in style, with furniture and fittings that were obviously expensive. There were a lot of neutral colours, and a steel and glass fireplace in the wall that functioned from both sides, in the living and dining rooms. She quite liked what she saw, and mused that if he added a few gentle touches, she'd have liked it a great deal more. Some more colourful books on the half-empty shelves, a painting or two on the pale walls, some green plants or flowers, would make all the difference.

After he arrived, he made them coffee, putting the shiny black mugs on the table between them. She indicated the envelope on one side. 'It's all there, and the conditions are quite clear. I read it through on the train.'

He nodded. 'He's bluffing, isn't he?'

'As far as I understand the wording, yes, he is.'

'It's stupid of him. The organizers will remember his name, and they'll be very reluctant to engage him in the future, unless he turns out to be another worldwide star. They don't like troublesome artists.' He looked at her and gave her a brief smile. 'Thanks for coming up; it will definitely save my bacon, and fry his.'

She held his glance. 'No problem. It would have been impossible if you'd been in New York or Vienna, but London is just a train journey away. I promised Bill I'd go in tomorrow to make up for lost time.'

He ran his hand through his hair. 'Must you? It's not fair.'

She smiled. 'If I pushed it, Bill would let me off. I don't mind, as long as it doesn't happen too often.' She took a sip of the coffee, checked the time, and got up. 'Thanks for the coffee. I'm going to catch the five o'clock train back.'

With one hand stuck in the pocket of his trousers and the other holding his mug, he asked, 'What will you do till then?'

'What do women do when they have time on their hands? They go shopping!'

'I was going to suggest we could go for a walk in the park, but if you'd rather go on a spending spree . . . '

She caught her breath because it was so unexpected. He was deliberately suggesting spending a little time together. Her hand went unconsciously to her throat. The slender shape of her fingers caught his attention, and he mused that she was very attractive in many ways.

Holly said, 'I think I'd like that.'

'Good. Some fresh air would do me good, too. I'm indoors too much; I miss having time to go for a proper walk.'

'Is there a park near here?'

'Five minutes away! Whenever I need to relax, I often find that a quick stroll there among the greenery does wonders.'

4

A few minutes later, they were taking a leisurely stroll around the park. It was still busy, with a school class playing cricket, lots of people relaxing in deck chairs, and elderly people strolling along the smooth pathways. Eventually, they stopped by a kiosk near the park entrance with a few wrought-iron tables and chairs. Ian ordered them tea and a couple of delicious homemade cakes.

She looked across the table and smiled. 'This is really nice. You forget that you're in the middle of London, sitting here. It's like being in the countryside, and this cream cake is super.'

Resting his elbows on the table and caressing his cup, he smiled. 'Yes, I agree. I love London, all the theatres and concerts . . . but it is nice to get away from it sometimes. A walk in this park is a real pick-up.'

She leaned back, nodding, and looked around. 'I don't know if I could live here permanently, though. It seems very vibrant and interesting, and all the museums and galleries and places of interest would always be a temptation, but there's also a sense of permanent urgency. People are always rushing around and have faces with hounded expression, as if the devil himself was after them.'

Ian laughed. 'You may be right. You have a very refreshing way of looking at the world.'

'I look at it in the same way you do, even though I am a few inches closer to the ground. Perhaps that makes all the difference.'

Smiling, he observed, 'Some parts of London have a friendly, sociable atmosphere, and others are totally anonymous. For some time now, I've been tempted to move to somewhere with a stronger community feeling. I'm just too lazy to make the effort. Simply finding something affordable is a Herculean task, and then there's all the work involved in actually moving and settling in ... I just don't have the time. I think if you analysed all big cities in the world, they all face the same kind of problems.'

The wind lifted Holly's hair and then restored it closely to the shape of her head again. Ian looked at her, and wondered if she realized what an attractive picture she made. His eyes slipped down her face and settled on her lips.

Her eyes narrowed as she looked up at the sun. 'I'm still glad that I live where I know everyone's name, and everyone knows me.' The memory of every other man she'd been with faded to nothingness as she chatted and studied Ian more closely. She had to be careful. Ian Travers was sophisticated, and could easily shake her contentment.

She reached for her cup. Ian's attention was drawn to her fingers again. They were strong and slim.

Holly drained her cup and returned it to the saucer. 'That was delicious and just what I needed. Thank you!'

The white of his teeth flashed briefly, and a stray breeze ruffled his hair. He looked young and relaxed. 'You're welcome. Would you like some more tea?'

She wrenched herself away from her preoccupation with him, and shook her head. 'No thanks! Do you look after your flat; do your own cooking?'

His lips twitched, but he said gravely, 'It's a service flat, and I seldom cook these days. I keep a stock of ready-made meals in the freezer. When my Mum was alive, her meat and two veg was my highlight of the week. You can't beat home cooking. Dad seems to live on pre-frozen meals, too.'

'He never needed to cook until your mother died, did he? I got him a very basic cookery book a while back. He's now managing things like shepherd's pie, sausage and mash, and spaghetti bolognese. He's trying to increase his repertoire. It's a good thing, because it means he has to shop. That gets him out of the house for a while.'

He nodded. 'Good. I'm glad. Having you there is an extra bonus. You keep an eye on him.'

She nodded. 'A bit! I hope he feels someone else is around if he needs them. Someone who is trying not to interfere too much.'

The smell of Ian's aftershave drifted across the table. She was pleased to find it was easy to share time with him. He might know all about the world of music, and have travelled far afield, but she found she was on equal footing when it came to books, politics, newspapers, or sport. He knew practically nothing about district happenings, but he was interested when she mentioned someone or something local. She was glad she loved reading and knew a lot about places he'd seen, even though she'd never been there. She could ask sensible questions and make coherent remarks.

'You're so lucky to have seen so much of the world.'

His eyes were soft and laughing. Ian could barely remember when he'd enjoyed himself more. She was a very down-to-earth person, who spoke her mind and was well-read. 'I'm not on holiday when I'm there; I'm working. Sometimes I never get beyond an airport hotel.' He ran his fingers through his thick hair. 'I suppose it is a shame, but business has priority, and time is money.'

She regarded him with a speculative gaze. 'I can understand that you don't have much spare time — but isn't it a shame to be in foreign surroundings, and not even enjoy a coffee at a sidewalk bistro to take in the atmosphere?'

His reserve began to dissolve, and he realized that for some reason just being here with Holly raised his spirits. It was a pleasure to relax and be himself for a change. Clients usually talked exclusively about their career, or their next performance. It was his job to reassure them and keep them happy. Most of the friends he knew in London didn't notice that they only talked about themselves all the time. Conversation rarely went beyond the world of music, art, or mutual acquaintances. Sometimes women openly signalled willingness for a bedroom adventure, but he was seldom tempted. If it happened, there was a mutual understanding that a night together meant nothing more to either of them.

He didn't feel happy when he thought about that, especially now when facing someone like Holly. He reminded himself that he had believed in loyalty and affection until his ex-fiancée had dropped him. Since then, no one had ever tempted him enough to think about a permanent arrangement.

Eyeing Holly across the table, he decided he really liked her. There was no comparison between someone from his home village who worked two jobs to earn a living wage, and nearly all the other women he met these days. His thoughts steadied. Holly undoubtedly expected the kind of love and companionship his parents had shared all their married life, but he knew that it didn't exist any more. Women were more demanding, and less conciliatory. He could live with ambition, but not callousness and insensitivity. A partnership was impossible unless you wanted the same things from life and would support each other. He was surprised, almost shocked, to find how Holly's honesty and goodness touched something inside that he'd forgotten existed. She was different, completely refreshing, and undemanding. She worked well, cared about other people, and was still an independent character.

Holly looked around. 'I like it here. Do you come often?'

He leaned back into his chair. 'Not as often as I'd like. When I'm in London, the weather isn't always as nice as it is today; and I imagine a lot of my guests would be surprised, to put it mildly, if I invited them to share a pot of tea and a cake from a kiosk.'

She played with her coffee spoon. 'Then they don't know what they're missing. Don't you get fed up with toadying to all these singers and musicians? I gather from what you say that you often have to.'

He laughed, and his even white teeth flashed for a moment. 'I don't 'toady' all the time, Holly. Only when it's the easiest way to calm someone down. And I do have some nice clients, but it's true that nearly all of them expect special treatment. I think, the higher they go, the less time they have to be real people. Unless they have a steady relationship or a loyal family in the background, they turn into people who'd sell their own grandmother for another lucrative contract. They often act unreasonably when they are crossed — but don't tell anyone I said that!'

Holly was so glad they'd spent these couple of hours together. Their interchange was sincere and candid. She tilted her head to the side. 'I don't think I could do what you do all the time.'

He nodded and chuckled. 'No, I don't suppose you could. You learn how to handle people, Holly! You learn that a lot of artists need insincere flattery just to be able to cope with their lives every day. I know it seems stupid and dishonest to outsiders — but remember that they spend most of their time on their own, moving from one performance to the next. I try to soft-soap as sparingly as I can. When I do praise, I try to be truthful. You can praise at all kinds of levels. Usually a couple of sensible words are enough to get them through a phase of indecision and uncertainty. I only praise someone to high heaven when they deserve it. I'm sure that most of my clients forget me ninety-nine percent of the time.'

'That's sad. I mean, if you work hard to match them to the right event, they ought to be more grateful.'

'Oh, they don't forget me completely — they call me when a problem crops up! But that's fair enough. There wouldn't be any point in having an agent if he just booked a performance and does nothing else. That would be boring. It's an interesting challenge to sort out the hiccups. I'm an agent, a mediator and an agony aunt. I wouldn't do it if I didn't like what I do.'

'I suppose not. Wouldn't you like to do less travelling, with regular hours and a permanent basis?'

He shrugged. 'I suppose I will slow down one day. I haven't given much thought to it so far. I've made a lot of contacts. I think I could back off and move down a level, if I wanted to. I could concentrate on organising local festivals in the UK, even pop concerts or other festivals. But on the whole, I enjoy what I'm doing at present, so I don't miss my hammock on the apple tree in the garden very much. The fact that I have a very efficient secretary has already reduced the pressure notice-ably.'

She coloured, but didn't comment. 'If you enjoy your work, that's all that matters, I suppose.'

He nodded. 'What about you? Are you happy with the combination of bookshop and my office work?'

'At the moment, yes; and it's so comfortable and lazy to live with my parents. And I'd so miss Josh — their dog — if I ever moved out! It has to change one day, though, for my own good. I must learn to stand on my own two feet. The main obstacle is the fact I like living in the village. It's all uncomplicated and very English. I like it.' She played with the crumbs on her plate and continued. 'I'm also pleased that your Dad has joined in village happenings recently. I think it's doing him good.'

He ran his hand down his face. 'To my shame, I must admit I haven't concerned myself enough with what he does. When my mother died, he was still working; so he was always busy and seemed to cope okay. When he took early retirement, I knew he must have more time on his hands, but somehow we never talked about it. I was always on the go, and he probably didn't want to bother me.'

'I gather that, and I think he was lonely for a while, but he keeps himself busy with various things nowadays.'

'I hope that now you're helping me with the office work, I can spend a bit more time with him when I'm home.'

She gave him a sudden smile. 'That would be great. I think he'd love that. He's very proud of you and what you've achieved, but I think he also feels left behind, because he can't relate to what you do.'

'I promise you that I'll make an effort.'

'Do. Your dad is a nice person.'

'Ian!' The sound of a woman's voice floated across to their table.

Holly looked around, trying to place it. Ian swivelled and looked too. Olivia de Noiret was on the other side of the railings, looking into the park. She hurried through the wrought-iron entrance gates and came towards their table.

Holly recognized her from the photos. In reality, she looked even more attractive, and was wearing a beautifully tailored slubbed-silk dress with a matching jacket in a lovely shade of pale lilac.

Ian was clearly surprised. He got up. 'Olivia. What are you doing here?'

A cloud of her perfume wafted in their direction. 'I just went to your flat, and the concierge told me you'd gone in this direction. I guessed you were coming here.' Her eyes skimmed over Holly, but returned to Ian's face again straight away.

He stood up and introduced them. 'Holly, this is Olivia de Noiret.'

Holly smiled. 'Hello! I'm pleased to meet you.'

Ian continued: 'This is Holly: she runs my office, and came up to London with a contract I need urgently for tomorrow morning.'

Without acknowledging Holly, Olivia gave him a suggestive smile and smoothed the jacket of her outfit. 'I've had a hell of a rehearsal this afternoon, and I thought we could have a drink together or go out for a meal to calm my nerves. That man is intimidating.'

Ian laughed softly. 'Lawrence has a reputation of getting the best out of his performers, so bear with it.'

'We can go back to your flat, can't we?'

Holly had the feeling she was in the way. She looked at her watch briefly. 'Please don't let me keep you any longer, Ian. It's almost time for me to catch the train.'

Lines crossed his forehead. 'There's no reason for you to rush off. I have to leave soon for my meeting as well. We can share a taxi.'

'I can take the Tube.'

'The least I can do is make sure you catch the train home with as little fuss as possible.' Looking at Olivia, he said, 'Sorry, but I doubt if I'll have time for anything this evening. I have a business meeting, and I don't know when it'll end.'

'Well you can at least walk me back to the flat, darling.'

Holly gathered her belongings together. She pushed her chair away with the back of her knees and stood up. She felt a little disappointed that their teatime had ended so abruptly. 'I have plenty of time to get to the station to catch my train. Don't worry about me.'

He looked slightly annoyed. 'Damn! I forgot my briefcase I have to go back to my flat for it! I'll get you a taxi.'

Before Holly could respond, he left them. The two women stood silently and avoided each other's glances. Holly didn't know what to say to Olivia, and Olivia didn't think for a single second that she could bridge the gap with some impersonal remark. Holly decided to follow Ian towards the entrance.

He was signalling to an approaching taxi when he caught sight of her. 'Thanks again for coming up, Holly.'

She gave him a smile. 'You're welcome. The taxi wasn't necessary, but if it makes you feel better . . . '

When the taxi pulled in, he handed the driver a couple of notes. 'Paddington!' The driver nodded and Holly got in.

Holly settled back into the upholstery, but couldn't help looking out of the rear window. Olivia had joined Ian, and Holly thought that he still looked irritated. He began to stride away in the direction of his flat. Olivia waited a moment, and then hurried after him as fast as her high heels allowed. He turned the corner and was lost to Holly's sight.

⋆ ⋆ ⋆

Looking unseeingly at the greenish-blue blur of the countryside as the train journey progressed, Holly wondered why it was so easy to recall his features. She'd enjoyed their meeting very much — until Olivia had ended it so abruptly. She recalled what he'd said about him pandering to the whims of top stars; but she had the feeling that, in Olivia de Noiret's case, she was someone who always expected special attention. And Ian didn't seem prepared to knuckle under. Olivia must meet lots of famous and interesting men in the course of her career every day; but, from the way she acted, it looked like her interest at the moment was firmly focused on Ian, and she was hoping for his exclusive attention.

Physically, they were a very attractive pair. Holly understood why she might be attracted to Ian. He was good-looking, intelligent, and his years as an agent handling world stars had given him a polish that was now inborn. Holly was surprised by his reaction to the famous opera star's requests just now. The feeling of awkwardness between the two of them was noticeable. The reason must be personal and not professional. Olivia's unexpected interruption and demands had irritated him. Holly had the impression she was trying to pressure him into a stronger relationship. If they were having an affair, she must realize he wasn't likely to give up his privacy just to keep her happy. If she'd walked past them this afternoon, and mentioned that she'd seen them later, Ian would have probably nodded and explained who Holly was, and there would have been no resulting negative atmosphere.

Leaning back into her seat, she remembered how his dad had talked about his former fiancée and how the disappointment had changed him. Perhaps he didn't believe in lasting relationships anymore. Especially if he thought someone was trying to control him.

They were almost at their destination. She'd promised Bill she'd help in the bookshop all day tomorrow, but she'd probably see Ian's dad on Sunday. She decided not to mention that Olivia had turned up unexpectedly. It wasn't important, and Ian's life was his own affair.

* * *

Holly was always busy in the office. She'd sorted out a couple of enquiries without his help this week. One came from a female singer who enthused about Ian, and tried to pick up personal information about him. She was unsuccessful. Ian phoned once, too, for some information that she had to search out from the piles still stacked on the floor. He sounded relaxed and quite happy. She heard that the problems over the contract had been sorted out. Holly wondered if the same applied to Olivia too, but she didn't ask.

Finding what he needed had taken her the best part of the afternoon, and it made Holly even more determined to get things sorted out as soon as possible. It was an awful waste of time, searching for items that should be stored in the filing cabinet — or, if they weren't official papers, in files in the bookcase.

She heard someone knocking on the door downstairs. She hesitated for a moment. No one apart from her parents and Bill knew she was here. Bill never knocked, and her parents usually phoned if they wanted something. It wasn't her cottage. It was probably someone trying to sell something. Millie came in once a week to clean, and she kept everything in tip-top condition, but she had her own key. Holly reminded herself that she was here to do office work, nothing else.

The knocking continued, and Holly decided it must be something important. She skipped downstairs and looked out of the small side window. There was a man with a small envelope in his hand. He was dressed in a courier's uniform, and there was a car outside the gate with the same logo on the side. She decided there was no danger. It might even be something important for Ian, like an urgent contract. Opening the door gingerly, she gave the man a tentative smile. 'Can I help you?'

The man looked bored. 'Afternoon! I have a registered envelope for someone called Ian Travers. He lives here, doesn't he?'

'Yes, but he's not here at the moment, I'm afraid. I'm not even sure if he's planning to come down this weekend. He's in London. He lives there most of the time.'

'Oh, Lord! What happens now? I'm paid to hand it over personally. I didn't know anything about him being in London. In fact, the address is actually next door's. The surname was the same, but the Christian name didn't match. I was about to take off when I had a look at this place and saw his name.' He ran his hand over his stubbly hair.

Holly was curious, but it wasn't really her job to pry into Ian's private life.

'The cottage next door belongs to Ian's father, and this one belongs to Ian, even though he spends most of his time in London. Perhaps you can leave the envelope with his father? It might solve your problem.'

He shook his head. 'There's no one in. I rang the bell a minute ago.'

'Oh yes, I forgot; he's gone out fishing this afternoon!' Holly opened the door wider.

After a short pause, he asked, 'And are you his wife? His girlfriend?'

'I'm his part-time secretary. I can give you his London address if you like.'

He shook his head. 'I'll have to take it back to local headquarters, and I'll get a mouthful from my boss for not delivering it. Could you sign for it?'

'I could, I suppose, but what if it is something that he needs to know about straight away?'

The man looked hopeful. 'Perhaps you or his dad can open it and read it to him over the phone?'

'Does it say who sent it?'

The man fumbled with the envelope, looking for a return address. 'Here it is. It's from someone called Juliette Keller. She paid the top rate to be certain he got it.'

5

Holly's expression lightened. 'Oh, well, I do recognize the name. She's an old friend of Mr Travers. I could sign for it and give it to his father, if that's allowed. Otherwise, I'm afraid you'll have to track him down in London.'

Relieved, the man smiled. 'That would be great. If you can sign here, please! You're obviously someone who will see that he gets it, and that's all I want.'

Holly reached out for the envelope. 'Where do I sign? I'll make sure he receives it. If he's not coming down on the weekend, I'll ask his dad to read the contents to him over the phone.' She waved him off and went back to her work.

She called next door when she was on her way home. Harry was back, and smiled when he opened the door.

'Hello, Holly! What can I do for you?'

Holly explained about the arrival of the registered letter. His brows drew together, but he said, 'Ian is coming down tomorrow. I'll remind him to look for it. He's bringing someone with him this time — Olivia de Noiret.'

'Really.' Holly wondered why she felt disappointed. 'What an honour for the village. That's if we see her, of course.'

Harry laughed gruffly. 'Your guess is as good as mine. I don't know what the plans are.'

'What about feeding her? Are you responsible?'

'Heaven forbid. I can hardly put shepherd's pie in front of such an illustrious guest, can I? Ian usually asks me to get the basic stuff in for him. I get the same things from Annie's shop every time he comes, but if he wants anything special he usually gets that himself. I already mentioned that he hasn't even invited anyone down here very often, haven't I? So she must be someone special.'

'Yes. Let's hope this good weather holds. I've left the letter on the coffee table in the living room. I didn't know if you were home, so I thought it was best to leave it there and not push it through your letterbox if you weren't in. If Ian is coming down, he'll see it there when he gets in.'

He nodded thoughtfully. 'Why don't you call in tomorrow, casually? Pretend you need something from the office, and meet Olivia.'

Holly didn't want to mention that she'd already met her, and wasn't anxious to do so again. 'No, I won't bother. You can tell me all about her on Monday. Enjoy yourself.' She gave him a warm smile and looked at her watch. 'There's a serial on the TV at eight o'clock; one of those dark Swedish ones. I'm going for a walk with Josh, and then watching the next episode.'

'You should get out more, Holly. You're too young to be a couch potato.'

'I'm not. Don't worry about me, I'm

fine. You know I'm not a partygoer by nature. I often meet up with friends for a meal or a natter, and I play indoor hockey and keep fit. I'm not desperate for a boyfriend, if that's what's worrying you. I'm happy with my life, Harry. Are you going anywhere this evening?'

Harry rubbed his chin. 'I'm going to see Sid. He promised me some rose cuttings. They would be real eye-catchers in that sunny corner down the bottom of the garden. The ones he has smell wonderful, too. A lot of the modern ones look fantastic but have no scent. A rose that doesn't smell isn't worth much in my eyes.'

Holly nodded. 'See you on Monday, then.'

'Yes, till Monday.'

Watching her departing figure, Harry was wistful. He thought about Juliette, and wondered what was in the envelope.

* * *

Holly hurried off. Minutes later, she was home, and had changed into jeans and a sweatshirt. Josh knew what to expect when she picked up his lead, and he couldn't imagine anything better than the occasional run. His fur waved in the breeze as he kept pace with her.

Holly ran slowly until she was outside the village. When she was sure there were no other animals in sight, she let Josh off the lead when she reached one of the fields. The dog was in seventh heaven as he chased imaginary insects. Holly tried to ignore the picture of Ian and Olivia snuggled together in his cottage over the weekend. Now that she'd met Olivia de Noiret, and knew how attractive she was, she wondered if she fitted in with Ian's lifestyle. She watched Josh, sighed, and wondered how Ian would react when he found Juliette's letter.

★   ★   ★

The weather on Saturday morning was perfect. Holly took Josh for a quick walk after breakfast, and then set off for an extra morning of work in the bookshop.

Bill's wife usually helped out on a Saturday, but she was visiting her mother in hospital in Dundee, so Bill had asked Holly to fill the gap. Saturdays were always his busiest day.

When the shop opened, it was quiet for an hour or so, and Holly spent the time restocking the shelves with the newest arrivals. Then a steady stream of customers began to wander around the various displays and shelves. Bill was soon busy advising, and manning the cash desk at the same time. Holly made herself useful wherever she was needed. She found that people tended to ask for help if they needed it; the majority of folk didn't like being interrupted, and Holly had learned to leave people alone until they requested assistance. Disturbing them didn't automatically mean increased sales.

She'd just helped a young mother and her little girl find a present for a schoolfriend's birthday party when Ian's voice drifted over her shoulder.

'Morning, Holly!'

She jumped, and colour flooded her cheeks. She was surprised to find him in the shop, and even more surprised to find Olivia de Noiret at his side. Olivia was tall, almost the same height as Ian. At the moment, her arm was tucked through at his elbow, and her red-tipped fingers rested possessively on his lower arm.

Holly hoped her voice was friendly enough. 'Morning, Ian. This is a surprise. What brings you into Abbey Combe?'

He looked around the shop. 'I thought you didn't work on Saturdays?'

'I don't, normally. I'm here this morning, because Bill's usual help is busy elsewhere.'

His blue eyes were relaxed and full of fun. 'So, this is where you work when you're not working for me. We've just arrived. I need a travel guide on Vienna. I've never been there. One with a map and details about transport, restaurants, and the like, if possible.' Remembering his companion, he turned slightly. 'Oh, Holly; you've already met Olivia, haven't you?'

Olivia was the epitome of sophistication. Her clothes were designer items: not too exotic in style, but clearly not off-the-peg. Her shoulder-length black hair swung with every movement of her head, and her make-up was faultless.

Holly held out her hand. 'Good morning, Miss Noiret, pleased to meet you again.'

Olivia didn't bother to untangle her arm from Ian's, or to offer the other one. She merely nodded.

Feeling a little snubbed, Holly let her hand fall to her side again, and hid her annoyance. If Ian noticed Olivia's rebuff, he gave no sign of it.

Olivia's perfectly arched eyebrows lifted as she asked, 'If you're Ian's secretary, why are you working in a bookshop?'

Trying not to show her irritation, Holly looked at her and managed a polite smile. 'The term 'secretary' is a bit of an exaggeration. Actually, I'm just his dogsbody, and try to keep things under control. He doesn't pay me much, so I need a second job to keep my head above water. This is it.'

Olivia looked at Ian's raised eyebrows, and noted his amused expression and how his eyes twinkled. Her own eyes narrowed as she considered Holly more carefully. She looked around the shop and plunged on carelessly. 'Oh, I see.'

Holly wondered for a moment if she was secretly hoping to be besieged by fans. No doubt there were lots of enthusiastic music lovers locally; but, as Olivia's visit was unannounced, busy Saturday shoppers weren't likely to give her any special attention. Even though she looked very sophisticated and elegant, lots of women these days managed to look almost as good as celebrities on a much more limited budget. Not everyone would have enough courage to walk up to a big name, either, even if they did recognize her.

Olivia waved her hand around. 'It all looks very cute and countrified, but it's not my scene. Are you actually buying something, Ian, or can we move on?'

Holly pulled herself together. 'Oh, yes.' She stared wordlessly at Ian for a moment. 'You wanted a travel guide. They're over here in the corner.' She led the way, and began searching the shelves for something suitable. Handing him three slim books, she explained: 'I expect you don't want anything too heavy. These are all intended to fit into your pocket. They're all good. I've never been to Vienna myself, but I'd recommend this one. It's from a very good travel series with all kinds of practical information like street plans, where to eat, transport routes, how to get to and from the airport, etcetera.' She waited as he flipped through some of the pages. It gave her the chance to study the firm set of his jaw and his face.

Olivia was bored, and eventually caught Ian's attention by commenting, 'I'm surprised that you've never been to Vienna, Ian. I've lost count of how many times I've appeared there.'

Buried in the pages, Ian looked up and surveyed the two women. His attention lingered longer on Holly in her knee-length skirt and pale blue blouse. He murmured, 'For some reason, until now, a personal visit has never cropped up. I've always managed to organize everything long-distance so far.' He kept the title Holly had recommended, and handed the others back. 'Yes, this does seem to have all I'll need for a short stay. I'll take it.'

Holly's eyes sparkled and she met his glance. 'The cash desk is over there. My boss Bill is behind the counter. Is that all, or do you want something else?'

'Well . . . where can I find a good butcher? Someone with good steak?'

'Try Walton's — it's further down the street, on the right. They get their meat from local farmers, and even if it is more expensive, the quality is great. My mum always buys her meat there. It's the best shop in town.'

'Town? You call this is a town? How quaint!' Olivia had found a way to join the tête-à-tête, and tittered.

Holly coloured, and said emphatically, 'Well, as far as I'm concerned, this is a town. As you'll see, Ian's cottage is in a small village.' She couldn't help adding, 'I live in the same village, and in comparison to there, this is a town. I think Ian understands what I mean.' Holly wondered why the other woman was acting with such obvious antagonism.

Olivia's eyes narrowed again, but she didn't reply. She hadn't liked how friendly and relaxed Ian had been with Holly that time she'd seen them together in London. The warmth between them was there again this morning. She needed to be careful, though, or she'd end up annoying Ian. She had to figure out what part this girl played in his life, and until then she couldn't afford to be too patronizing.

'Ian, can we go? This bookshop is undoubtedly fascinating, but I'm longing for a vodka and lime.'

Sounding somewhat exasperated, Ian eyed her. 'You insisted you wanted to find out where I go on the weekends. I told you the locality is a still backwater. Don't start complicating things, Olivia. I have to cater for myself when I come home; I don't have a servant at my beck and call to do the work for me, like you do.'

Holly pretended to tidy the nearby shelf and tried not to pay any attention.

Olivia ran one red-tipped finger down the side of his jaw. 'Oh, come on, darling. You know how I had to juggle my schedule for the next two weeks to get this weekend free. I didn't imagine I'd spend it doing shopping in the high street.'

Moving his head away, Ian looked

annoyed. 'If you can do without food for two days, we can drive straight home. I don't have any lime either, so we have to shop for that as well, or do without. Don't play the diva with me, Olivia; it won't work.'

Holly was a fascinated listener. Olivia suddenly remembered she was nearby. Red spots appeared on her cheeks, and her almond-shaped dark eyes glittered dangerously. Her generous red mouth was a straight line, and she disentangled her arm from his. 'I'm going back to the car. I'm sure you'll manage all this fascinating shopping much faster without me.'

Ian shrugged, handed her the keys, and warned her: 'A good idea. And don't get any ideas about leaving me stranded without transport. I'll join you as soon as I can.'

Without replying, Olivia grabbed the keys, did an about turn and hurried off towards the exit. Ian gave Holly a philosophical shrug and murmured, 'Artists are all performers from daybreak till midnight.' He paused and noticed the guide in his hands again. 'Right, I'll pay for this and be on my way. Thanks, Holly. I'd better hurry, otherwise Olivia really will drive my car into the next ditch.'

Holly laughed softly. 'Ah, well; she's hypersensitive, and I expect she likes the limelight. She'll enjoy her stay once she relaxes.'

He tilted his head to the side and snorted. 'Chance would be a fine thing. Olivia grew up in the centre of Geneva. I don't think she knows the meaning of the word 'countryside'. She probably expects cows to be lilac, and the sun to always shine.' He turned and lifted his hand in farewell as he made his way towards the cash desk.

Holly replaced the guidebooks and tried not to think about Ian and Olivia. Olivia was not right for him. He was single-minded, and she was also a demanding character. They didn't show much loving affection, either. She noted that Olivia sought physical contact but he didn't. On the other hand, some people kept their private feelings hidden, and she imagined Ian was like that.

Holly sighed. Perhaps she was just too unsophisticated to understand. People like Ian and Olivia weren't the normal kind of folk she came into contact with. They were both challenging personalities. Olivia had an explosive, artistic temperament, and Ian could close up like a clam when he wanted to. She suddenly remembered she'd forgotten to mention Juliette's letter. She'd had the perfect chance after Olivia left, but she'd forgotten all about it. Pushing her hair off her brow, she glanced around for a customer with a puzzled look on their face.

★ ★ ★

On Saturday evening, Holly called in at the Fox and Hounds on her way home after going to the pictures with her friend Gillian. She knew that her dad usually called in for a pint if it was his turn to take Josh for a walk. A wave of cheery noise met her when she opened the door. It was always busy on a Saturday, and today was no exception. She pushed the hair off her face and searched the crowd for her father. He was on the far side of the low-beamed room, talking to some cronies. She couldn't see their dog — but, as Josh was a Westie, that wasn't unexpected. He'd probably found himself a spot out of the way of people's feet.

Holly started to make her way through. Someone called her name above the din. Looking around, she spotted Ian with his father and Olivia. They were huddled round a small table near the open fireplace. She nodded and smiled, hoping that would suffice, but Harry beckoned her over.

Harry looked pleased to see her. She couldn't tell from Ian's expression what he thought, but Olivia was bored. Overcrowded country pubs were not to her liking. Even if anyone here recognized her, people were too busy enjoying themselves to give her any special attention.

Holly concentrated on Harry, and gave him a smile while unbuttoning her red jacket. 'Hello! Enjoying a pint?'

He smiled and lifted his glass. 'Ian and Olivia decided to join me.'

'So I see.' Her glance swept across the room before returning to the other two seated at the table. She tried to ignore Olivia's designer clothes, and how her arm was hooked through Ian's.

Ian commented, 'You'll have to fight to get to the bar. It's been packed like this all night. Join us. I'll get you something.'

'No, thanks. My dad is over there, with some friends. I've been to the pictures, and called in on the off-chance that he was here. I'm going to join them for a drink.'

He nodded silently.

'Enjoy yourselves. See you on Monday, Harry.' She left them and shoved her way through the throng gathering around the bar. She greeted some people on the way, and reached her father. He smiled when he saw her and pecked her cheek. Carl Jenkins, standing next to him, ran the local repair shop. He threw his arm round her shoulder. Her Dad signalled to the barkeeper and ordered her a lager.

Carl asked, 'Where have you been, my darling?'

'The pictures. Saw a good film. It was called *Seven Steps to Hell*. Have you seen it?'

'Haven't been to the pictures for months, I'm not much of a film-goer. On the other hand, if you come with me, I might change my mind about that.'

She looked up at him and smiled. 'Is this your method of asking for a date, by any chance? Forget it! You have a rotten reputation, Carl.'

Carl tilted his head to the side. 'It's lies; all lies. For you, I would turn over a new leaf.'

'If the rumours are true, that would be impossible. You've been at it too long.'

Carl ruffled her hair and laughed. Her dad handed her a glass of lager and she took a welcome sip. They were among a group of their neighbours gathered in a tight cluster. The usual kind of gossiping took place — discussions about local burglaries and the football results. Holly couldn't help looking for Ian and the others through the gaps. When her eyes locked with his for a second, she sensed he wasn't happy. Perhaps it was just because of the noise and activity going on around them. Harry also looked like he'd rather be with the rest of the neighbours, and Olivia looked fed up. Holly looked away quickly, and concentrated on the people nearby.

By the time she'd finished her drink and her dad said he was ready to go, Ian's table was empty. Holly picked Josh up from where he'd stretched out at their feet. There was a good chance someone would tread on him if she left him to find his own way out between all the legs.

When they'd nearly reached the door, she mentioned to her father, 'Harry was here. He was over there with Ian and Olivia de Noiret.'

'Yes, I had a word with him when I came in. I think he would have rather joined us for a pint at the bar. That woman is good-looking, but she's also snobbish. Harry realizes that too, but what can he do?'

'Then it's a pity he didn't come with Ian and leave her at home. Ian told me he hadn't had enough time to share things with his dad for ages, because there was always work waiting for him when he came home. Now that I'm helping in his office, he does have time for things like a quick trip down the pub at last. Pity that he had to include her this evening.'

'Are they a couple? They are both from the world of the rich and famous.'

She shrugged. 'I don't know. She

seems to fancy Ian, but I can't figure out how he feels about her.'

At last, they were outside in the fresh air. Holly put Josh down, and he was delighted to be checking foreign smells every inch of the way. The trio strolled companionably through the silent streets in the direction of their cottage.

'Harry once told me that Ian was engaged to a famous cellist called Juliette Keller. Do you remember her?'

Her father was silent for a moment. 'Yes, that's true. I'd almost forgotten about that. We never saw her much. I think it more or less all happened a couple of years after we moved here. I remember the headlines in the newspapers at the time, and how reporters surrounded Harry's cottage. Their engagement ended in a blaze of publicity because she'd been hailed as the next star cellist. She agreed to tour with one of those pop bands, probably intended as a publicity gag, but it went wrong. She broke her engagement. She also gave up her aspiration to be a world-renowned cellist later on. I wonder where she is now?

'I think she's still with David Allydyce. He was a member of that pop group. She must have fallen for him badly, because a lot of water has flowed under the bridge since then, and those two are still together.'

Her father threw his arm round her shoulders and gave her a hug. 'I'm so glad we have you and your brother, and you've always been so sensible.'

6

Harry came into the bookshop on Monday morning just before they closed for lunch. The old-fashioned bell over the door tinkled when he entered. Bill was tidying the shelves.

Harry nodded towards the rooms at the rear. 'Can I go straight through?'

Bill was used to Harry coming in to see Holly whenever he came into town, and he and Harry had also developed a friendship. They supported the same football team.

'Yes, go ahead. Tell Holly to put the kettle on. I'll come through in a couple of minutes; there's nothing much happening here any more. It's almost time for lunch anyway. I'll put this lot on the shelves and join you.'

Harry fought his way through a narrow passageway — rendered even narrower by Bill's habit of piling ordered books along the walls. The wooden planking had seen better days, and Holly had been trying to persuade Bill to move everything out of the way so that she could give it a scrub — its first in decades. Bill had brushed her suggestion aside. He insisted he liked it the way it was. He compared it to a patina, and said that if Holly cleaned things up too much, some of the atmosphere of the shop would flow down the drain with the dirty water. She thought differently.

Apart from the area around Holly's desk, the back office had a dusty, overloaded and untidy look. Holly was glad that customers never saw what the room looked like. Some of them would take instant flight and never return.

Holly smiled when she saw him. 'Hi Harry, what brings you into town this morning?'

'I had to go to the chemist's, and thought I'd pop in and see you. Now I'm here!'

'Anything the matter?'

'No, nothing special. My blood pressure is too high, but it hasn't been normal for years. I get tablets to keep things under control. Old Dalton won't give me a prescription unless I go in for a check-up now and then. I'd run out, and just managed to get a new prescription before he finished surgery last Friday. But I forgot to get it filled straight away, and had to come back in for the tablets again today.'

Holly viewed his friendly face and twinkling blue eyes; now that she'd met his son a couple of times, she could see that Ian had his father's eyes. 'I hope you remember to take them regularly.'

'Oh, don't you start fussing too! My Margery used to fuss all the time about me taking them.'

'Well, do you?'

'I'm supposed to take one morning and evening, but I must admit, sometimes I forget whether I have or not. I don't suppose it makes that much difference.'

Frowning, Holly said, 'It does,

otherwise you wouldn't need to take them, would you? There are plastic containers with little compartments that you can fill ready for the whole week, and then you can see at a glance if you've taken your dose or not. I'll bring you one from the chemist's if you like. My mum has one for her thyroid tablets. She swears by it, and it works like a charm for her.'

Scratching his head, he nodded. 'Yes, alright. Next time you go in for something, buy me one. What about a cup of coffee? Bill said he'd join us in a minute.'

Holly got up. 'Honestly, sometimes I think this place is a more of a bistro café than a bookshop. I spend more time making coffee than I do working, some mornings.'

His eyes sparkled. 'And you love it.'

Holly laughed and filled the kettle. 'What do you think about Olivia now that you've met her?'

He reached for a biscuit. 'Ian introduced us on Saturday morning when I was pottering in the garden. He was setting up the grill. I only chatted to them briefly over the fence. I did remember to mention the letter from Juliette. Olivia butted in and said she'd found it and already given it to Ian. I wondered if she'd read it without his permission, because he didn't seem very happy.'

Holly bit her lip. 'Oh! I should have warned him, but I forgot. I didn't reckon with him bringing a visitor. Was he upset?'

'About the contents? It's hard to tell. You know Ian. He keeps his cards close to his chest, and I'm positive he would never talk to me about Juliette in front of a stranger. It all happened years ago, and hardly anyone remembers they were engaged. If he wants to tell me what it's all about, he'll do so. There's no point in pushing Ian, it has the reverse effect.'

'Didn't they invite you to join them for their barbeque?'

'Yes, he did; but this fad for

barbequing morning, noon and night is not up my street. She smiled at me when I refused, but I had the feeling it was only faked. She wanted to be alone with Ian. I didn't mind. I have better things to do with my time during the day than watching Ian grill sausages. I refused politely, and left them to it. I went with them to the pub later on that evening, but you saw us there, didn't you?'

'What do you think of her?'

He shrugged. 'Hard to say. She smiles a lot, but the smiles are too practised and artificial. I think she was making an effort to be civil because I was Ian's dad, but I think it's all part of a performance. Somehow, I don't think she makes much effort to be congenial to anyone, unless there's something in it for herself. The only time she looked focused and alert was when she told me where she was due to perform next week. She expects everyone to be interested in that.'

Holly spooned instant coffee into

some mugs and nodded. 'I met them too, on Saturday. Ian came in to buy a travel guide. Perhaps we shouldn't be too critical, but I also have my reservations about her. She was bored . . . but, from what Ian tells me, all artists are touchy and introverted. If she's an example of the clients he handles, Ian doesn't have an easy job.'

He nodded. 'Yes, he often says many of them are difficult beings; but that some of them are also decent and easy to handle. I could always tell by the way they talked on the telephone if they were difficult or not.'

Holly nodded and handed him a mug. 'Yes, I've noticed that too. Sometimes they're rude, and they're almost always demanding, but I make them understand they have to treat the person on the other end of the line like a human being too. Mostly they calm down after that.'

Harry laughed gruffly and took a sip. Cupping his hand round the mug and sticking one thumb through the handle, he continued. 'Anyway, Miss de Noiret didn't stay long. I was round the other side of the house tying up the lupins on Sunday morning, when I heard a loud exchange and then some doors banging. Ian was outside reading next time I saw him, and when I asked where Olivia was, he said he'd just given her a lift to the railway station and she was catching the next train back to London.'

Holly didn't understand why she felt relieved. It was probably because she'd decided Ian deserved someone better than an egotistical performer who believed she was the centre of the universe. 'And he stayed?'

'He left hours later. He came across, saying he was leaving. He had an appointment in Manchester the next day, and I think he went straight there from here. We had a cup of tea in the garden. I didn't mention Juliette or Olivia, and he didn't offer any additional information.'

The sound of plodding feet announced that Bill was approaching. Holly got up to pour some hot water on the coffee grains. Bill breezed into the office, proceeded to sink down into Holly's chair, accepted the cup, and held it while she added the desired amount of sugar.

'Did you see the match on Saturday? I saw the summary of it later in the sports show. Chelsea wiped the floor with them, didn't they?'

Holly accepted her fate, and made herself comfortable in the other, slightly wonky, chair in the room. She shut out the two men's discussions about penalties, fouls, and stolen goals, and allowed herself to think about other things.

When she got to the office later that afternoon, Holly felt a little disappointed when she found there was no note from Ian. She got on with sorting and filing, feeling satisfied when she saw how well the office system was beginning to take shape. She started to enter Ian's latest expenditures into the appropriate bookkeeping account.

By Thursday, she could see a real light at the end of the tunnel, and she even began to wonder how she'd fill her time once everything had been checked, filed and regulated. She hadn't seen Harry since Monday morning, and he hadn't even shared her tea breaks. He was okay, though, because she saw him in and around the cottage when she passed: busy with other activities. It gave her uninterrupted afternoons to get on with everything, and she was glad he was occupied, and not listless in the way he'd been shortly after his wife's death.

* * *

A few days later, Holly was still busy. She'd had a couple of calls this week, and Ian had phoned once for some detailed information about one of the contracts. She'd been reduced to searching the remaining piles on the floor in the end. It had taken her the best part of the afternoon to find what he needed, and it made her even more determined to get things properly filed as soon as possible. It was a awful waste of time, searching all over the place for items that should be in the filing cabinet. She was already looking forward to the weekend, and had decided to be reckless — to spend some of the extra money she was now earning on a pair of stunning shoes she'd seen in a shop window in town.

She was busy sorting through another one of the dusty piles when she found a newspaper cutting of an interview Ian had given to a local newspaper three years ago. She read it with interest, and particularly liked how he showed his attitude to his job via the words he used. He was asked: *'What's the best thing about your job?'* He'd answered: *'The audience's reaction to a great performance.'* Then came: *'What's the worst thing about your job?'* And his reply: *'Having to trawl through a pile of untalented people to find the great ones.'*

The phone rang and interrupted her reading. Something quivered inside for a moment when she heard his voice.

'Holly? Ian here. How are things?'

She brushed her hair out of her eyes and sat down on the carpet. 'Fine. No problem. Did your meeting work out?'

'Umm!'

Holly hesitated for a moment. 'Ian, I'm sorry that I left that letter from Juliette Keller on the table. I should have warned you, but I forgot about it when you were in the shop, and I didn't reckon on your visitor seeing it, either.'

'Don't worry. It certainly wasn't polite of Olivia to pick it up and read it, either.' He hesitated. 'Juliette's sent me an invitation to her wedding.' Another pause. 'I don't know why. We have met briefly now and then at parties and other events after we broke up, but she belongs to another world now, and life has gone on without her. I'm undecided about whether to go or not. I presume you know all about Juliette?'

'Your dad told me about her, and what happened. I don't remember her.'

'The invitation is for me and a plus-one. Perhaps she wants to show me what I've missed out on.' He sounded cynical.

'Do you . . . still care? Perhaps it's her way of making peace with the past.'

'Heavens, no! I realize now it would have been a mistake. If it hadn't been David Allydyce, it would have been someone else. She was too young to know her own mind, and her talents and enthusiasm blinded me to the truth.'

'And that was?'

'That we mistook friendship and similar interests for love. The backlash has made me very distrustful and sceptical about what the word 'love' actually means, though. Apparently, she's pregnant, and they want to get married and make it all official before the baby is born. Just a registry do, and drinks after.'

'Well, at least she seems to have made

the right choice if they're still together years later.'

He laughed softly. 'Yes, that's true. We wouldn't have lasted. Pity about throwing all her talent away, though.'

'Ask your dad to go with you. He knew her, and he will be a good support.'

'Holly! What will that look like? Me turning up with my father at my ex-fiancée's wedding? Everyone goes with a real partner. I'll write and tell her I'm too busy.'

Holly was exasperated. 'And she'll see through that straight away. She'll know you're avoiding her. Isn't there someone else who'd go with you?'

'It's not so easy to ask anyone to partner you to a wedding when they don't know the persons involved.'

She didn't hesitate. 'I'll come with you, if you like.'

There was surprise in his voice. 'You will? Why should you?'

'Why not? I don't know her, but if you don't mind, and the situation doesn't bother you any more, I think it would be good for you and her to draw a line under the whole thing. By going, you'd be showing her that, as far as you're concerned, the past is gone and buried. Perhaps that is what she wants. Women on their wedding days like things to be all cut and dried. She definitely doesn't hate you, otherwise you wouldn't have received an invitation. I'll come — but only if you want me to, of course.'

His voice held a tinge of hope. 'It's this weekend. Is that okay with you?'

'Yes, it's okay.'

'It's very good of you. I was just about to send a thank-you note and make my excuses. I'll tell her I'm coming with a friend instead. They've arranged things at a local registry office near Juliette's parents' home — to avoid publicity. It's kind of you, Holly. It will make what could be an awkward task for me a lot easier.'

* * *

Holly walked to Ian's cottage. She met Harry. He was about to leave to help a friend with an application for a wheelchair. Harry knew she was going with Ian to the wedding. He gave her a speculative look, and then nodded. 'Good. I'm glad you're going to be with him. It's strange that she invited him, but she'll see he isn't pining for her any more. You look lovely.'

Holly went inside Ian's cottage to wait.

He arrived in plenty of time, looking very formal in his dark suit, lilac tie, and white shirt. She'd bought an expensive floral dress less than a year ago for a friend's wedding, so it fitted this occasion perfectly. The style was very simple, very classical, and very attractive.

It was too warm for a coat, so Holly had just added a short, lightweight jacket, and a chain-strap shoulder bag. Ian gave her special attention as he opened the door and got into his car. 'You look very smart this morning.'

Holly smiled. 'So do you. Sometimes it's a real pleasure to dress up now and then. It doesn't make sense really, does it?'

He started the engine and they moved off. 'No, but we're showing the other person extra respect, and putting ourselves in the right frame of mind for a special day. Women love weddings. It gives them a chance to splurge.' Looking sideways, he said, 'I like the outfit you've chosen. Very stylish, and the colour suits you, too.'

She coloured slightly. 'Did you have to reorganize work much? It was fairly short notice, wasn't it?'

He nodded. 'I postponed a couple of things today, and I have to fly to Oslo tomorrow. There's a Grieg festival planned for November and they're looking for performers. I'm going to try to push some of ours.'

Holly liked the way he mentioned 'ours' — it was almost as if she was really part of his business. She settled back into the leather seat and watched the passing scenery with half an eye. Buttercups still plastered the fields as they passed, and she noticed once how the sound of their passing car startled some pigeons into the thick greenery of a group of nearby trees.

'Your job keeps you on the move all the time, doesn't it? Don't you get fed up?'

Ian smiled. 'It's not as bad as it seems. Long-haul journeys are a bit of a drag because there is always jetlag to cope with. Sometimes the business is just for a day or two, and it takes a while to adjust because of flying both ways in such a short time. You do get used to it, but never completely. Meetings in Europe or within the UK aren't a problem.'

'It's a nice way to see some of the world, though.'

'If you spend most of your time between the airport or your hotel, you don't see much of anything. It sounds more glamorous than it is. I do add an extra day if it's somewhere new or special.'

Holly patted her hair. 'I've been to Paris for a couple of days, the Costa Brava on holiday with a friend of mine, and I went on a coach trip to Austria last year. I've never had enough money to travel to all the places I dream about. Perhaps I'll see some of them one day, though.'

'Where would you like to go?'

'New York, Australia, Paris again — it was fab — Tuscany, Israel, Greece, Hong Kong.'

He laughed softly. 'Why don't you just say 'everywhere'?'

She looked across and smiled. 'Everywhere!'

'I'm sure you'll see some of them if you are determined enough, and things like marriage and children don't trip you up too soon.'

'I won't be able to go very far on what you pay me!'

He burst out laughing, and was then silent for a moment. 'I'm really glad you offered to come with me this morning, Holly.'

She coloured, and her eyes twinkled in answer.

7

Time passed quickly and they made good progress. Holly longed to ask Ian about Juliette and what he really felt about her these days. She didn't have enough courage to do so. He chatted about a play he'd seen in London one evening, asked about her parents, and they talked about a recent bestseller that they'd both read.

When they reached their destination, a small country town, they left the car opposite the most imposing building they could see, and asked a passer-by where to find the registry office. The man, out with his dog, pointed them in the right direction, down a cobbled side-street.

Ian checked his watch. 'We have plenty of time.'

Holly straightened her dress and walked alongside him. On reaching an arched entrance into a medieval building, they saw there was a small bunch of people already gathered outside. They joined them, and Ian went straight towards a middle-aged couple at the centre of the gathering. Holly tagged along behind him. She presumed they were Juliette's parents, because they smiled, and Ian kissed the woman's cheek.

'This is my friend Holly.'

Juliette's mother and the grey-haired man at her side nodded. 'We're very pleased that you've come, Ian. It shows us that there are no bad feelings anymore.'

Some of the others looked at them curiously. They probably all knew who Ian was and what role Juliette had played in his life.

As they waited for the bride and groom to arrive, she wondered if he was thinking of the good times he'd shared with Juliette, and regretting things. If they'd been engaged, there must have been good times.

A Rolls Royce decorated with white ribbons arrived, and Juliette got out with her husband-to-be. He wore a white suit and a pale blue shirt open at the neck. Juliette wore a matching pale-blue trouser suit and white accessories. She was pretty, with dark hair and bright blue eyes. Her smiling face skimmed the group, and her smile widened when she saw Ian. He gave her a nod. Amid much ribaldry, they went inside.

Half an hour later, everyone followed the bridal pair to a nearby inn, where champagne and titbits were set out on bistro tables throughout the room. Flowers gave the room a festive appearance, and Juliette and David made the rounds of their guests. Ian had chatted to someone for a few minutes when they arrived, and Holly felt a little lost, because she knew no one and she wasn't used to making small talk with complete strangers.

When Ian returned to her side, he said, 'Sorry about that. That was

Juliette's brother Colin — the tall, thin man with reddish hair. He's a decent chap. Works for an engineering company. I always liked him. It was good to exchange news. This must be very boring for you.'

'No problem. I didn't expect anything different.'

Juliette and David reached them. Juliette looked up at Ian. 'Thank you for coming, Ian. It means a lot to me.'

David had his arm around her waist. 'Yes, thanks. It can't have been easy for you.' His soft brown eyes twinkled with a mixture of sympathy and cheekiness. Holly understood the fascination Juliette had felt when she met him.

Ian brushed her words aside. 'Thank Holly. This is Holly. She persuaded me it was the right thing to do.'

Juliette viewed Holly with heightened interest. 'Hi, Holly. It's nice to meet you.'

Holly nodded. 'Hi, and thanks for letting me come with Ian.'

'Our pleasure. It looks like Ian has

found someone worthwhile at last.'

Holly laughed softly. 'Can anyone tell if someone is okay, or not, that fast?'

'Ever since I met David, I've discovered I can pick out genuinely decent people from the crowd. I can't explain how or why, it just works.'

David laughed. 'It's true. She helps me to keep my balance. I rely on her to steer me clear of the wrong types.'

Someone called to them from across the room. Juliette reached up and kissed Ian's cheek. 'No more hard feelings?'

Ian shook his head. 'No.'

Holly felt a lump in her throat.

'Good. You and Holly must come and visit us.'

David dragged her away.

After some minutes more, and after Ian had chatted more to Juliette's parents, he said, 'I think we've done our duty. I'm ready to go. You too?'

Holly nodded.

They made their way through the rest of the people. Ian lifted his hand in farewell to Juliette and David, and they were soon out in the fresh air again.

He pulled at his tie. 'It wasn't as difficult as I expected. Thanks again for coming, Holly.'

He opened the door for her to get into the passenger seat, and looked at his watch. 'There's a nice restaurant not far from here. Let's have a good lunch before we go back.'

Holly nodded. The prospect pleased her, and she settled into the leather seat again. They were both quiet, their thoughts still busy with Juliette and her wedding.

Less than a half an hour later, they drove into the forecourt of a half-timbered black-and-white hostelry. It was relatively quiet. They were allotted a table overlooking the gardens. The ceiling had low beams and the walls were painted a soft apricot colour. It felt comfortable and welcoming. A few simple but stunning decorative effects gave the room just the right amount of elegance. It was a bright day, full of sunshine. The grounds ran down to some shallow banks and a peacefully flowing river. There were willow trees, groups of strategically placed chairs, and splashes of coloured flowers planted cleverly for the best effect.

Holly looked around. 'This is a very nice place.'

Seeing the approaching waiter, Ian said quickly, 'Chose whatever you fancy.'

The waiter handed them the menus. They both spent a little time studying them, and made their choices. Ian ordered some wine, and nodded when he tasted it.

'I can afford one glass even though I'm driving, but I hope you'll drink more if you feel like it.'

Trying to lighten the conversation, she remarked, 'Are you trying to get me drunk?'

He smiled, and his even white teeth flashed momentarily. 'No. Even if you were tipsy, it wouldn't matter, would it? I can still get you home safely.'

Holly found his face was irresistible:

the square chin, prominent cheekbones and blue eyes created a very unusual and attractive man. She shook her head. 'But you'll agree that it wouldn't be exactly praiseworthy to leave me on my parents' doorstep in a state of intoxication, wouldn't you? Have you been here before?'

'A few times, whenever I was on my way to Glyndebourne. They have a couple of rooms. The service is always excellent, and it's very peaceful here.'

Looking at the garden, she said, 'I bet.'

The waiter arrived with Holly's salad and Ian's soup. Throughout the meal, the conversation flowed and drifted — about music, Harry, the village, hobbies . . . As she'd already suspected, Ian didn't have much time for hobbies, but they shared a love of reading. She was also pleased to find he was interested in history, and enjoyed visiting tourist attractions and places of interest, although he had little time for such things these days.

Holly felt very comfortable with him, and she could tell he felt relaxed with her too. Perhaps it was because they were both free from emotional involvement. They were two people who could spend time together without worrying about the usual kind of niceties, or about what the other one really thought all the time.

*   *   *

When they reached home, Holly looked at her watch. 'I'll take Josh for a walk. It's still lovely weather.'

He gave her a lopsided grin and laughed softly. 'I hope you enjoy your walk with your dog; in fact, I almost envy him.'

She looked at him for a moment, and her heart skipped a beat or two. He was a shrewd businessman, but he was also a very outgoing and likeable person when he chose to be. She nodded. 'You'll be in touch?'

'Of course. Thanks again, Holly.

You've helped me to well and truly bury any remaining ghosts today.'

She hoisted her bag. 'You're welcome. I'm glad if I've helped.' She gave him a smile, and opened the car door.

Harry came out of his cottage when she passed, and she waved. When she looked back, he was leaning down to talk to Ian, still sitting in the car.

* * *

Next time Ian phoned, he asked, 'What are you doing?'

'You mean now, at this minute?'

'Yes.'

'I'm sitting on the carpet, sorting through one of the neglected piles of papers. I'll need a shower when I've finished. My hands are filthy.'

He laughed softly. 'It's all in a good cause. Being able to find what I need every time I open the filing cabinet is almost reality at last.'

'I'm not finished yet, but I will be — some time very soon.'

'Good. I'm calling to ask you to type me out a contract and have it ready when I come down on the weekend, please. Use the contract I had with Umberto Cavallo as a prototype. Just leave the appropriate spots for the fees and the dates empty, and copy the rest.'

Holly reached up to the desk and scrabbled around for a pencil. She noted the name on the paper in her lap. 'Umberto Cavallo?'

'Yes, that's right. You are worth your weight in gold, Holly. It's such a relief to know that when I do come home that I don't have to spend all my time in that office. Any other news I should know about? Anyone called?'

'Only the cellist, David Osborne. He phoned yesterday afternoon. He wanted to know if you've settled that engagement with the symphony concert in Bath. I sent you a text about it.'

'Yes, I remember. Good that you reminded me. I'll get in touch with him, promise.'

'He sounds nice, and he has a lovely voice.'

'Think so? Yes, I suppose David is a decent chap. Fame hasn't ruined him yet, and he's a very talented and promising cellist. He's already done a couple of mini-tours in Japan and Sweden.' There was a short pause. 'I gather you had a chat with him?'

'Yes, and I don't think he was fishing for special attention. He was just being nice. He even said he'd send me some complimentary tickets next time he plays locally, if I was interested.'

Sounding slightly impatient, he said, 'If you want tickets to any performances where our artists are appearing, just let me know.'

Hearing the irritation in his voice, she said, 'He wasn't trying to bribe me, Ian.'

'I didn't say he was. I just mean it's better if you get any free tickets from me. Usually I can always get complimentary ones quite easily.'

'I'll tell you what I told him. If I want

to go to a concert, I'll pay for my own ticket. I don't want to be beholden to anyone for anything.'

He was silent, then added brusquely, 'Perhaps I'll see you on the weekend?'

'I doubt it. Our paths never crossed on the weekend before, did they? Why should that change all of a sudden? Or did you want to see me about something to do with the office? Then I'll come in, of course.'

'No. That's not necessary. Now that you've almost eliminated the drudgery of searching for everything, it means I have time to do other things, like going for a walk, or down the pub with Dad.'

'That's a great idea. Your father is really pleased that he sees more of you these days.'

'That's my intention. Oh! Will you please tell Dad that Olivia de Noiret will be coming down with me again? She's been fishing for another invitation even though she had a tantrum last time. I'm hoping this is will be the last time she thinks about visiting. I don't know why the countryside is suddenly so attractive to her, especially after her abrupt departure last time. I've given up trying to understand her. I've given in, and hope she doesn't explode again.'

Holly imagined what Olivia's motives were, and wondered why she felt deflated. 'Oh! Yes, of course. I'll pass the message on.'

'Right. That was it.'

'I'll leave the contract on the desk for you.'

'Fine. Goodnight, Holly.'

She looked out of the window; it was still broad daylight, but he could be anywhere in the world, and have forgotten about the time difference. 'Bye!'

She called in at his cottage to tell Harry that Ian was coming, and bringing Olivia with him on her way home. Harry didn't look very pleased, but if Olivia was going to turn up more often, he'd have to get used to it.

Harry scratched his head. 'I'll keep out of the way as much as I can. I certainly won't be making a trip to the pub with them, like I did last time.'

'Coward! You should always welcome Ian's girlfriends.'

* * *

Holly didn't see them over the weekend, and she wasn't sorry that she hadn't. The idea of Olivia and Ian spending a passionate couple of days in his cottage annoyed her more than she cared to admit, but she pushed it to the corners of her brain. She arranged to go out with her best friend Saturday evening and her friend's chatter about her latest boyfriend went a long way to distracting her from stupid thoughts about her employer.

When she turned up for work on Monday, there was no note from Ian. Holly had always avoided going into Ian's private rooms, apart from to get water from the kitchen or use the toilet. She was careful to avoid any of the other rooms. She didn't even know how they were furnished. She deliberately didn't ask Millie any questions about Ian or the cottage if she met her.

She was just about to leave when the phone rang. She looked at the wall clock and shrugged as she picked up the receiver and a familiar voice snapped, 'Hello, this is Olivia de Noiret. Is that Ian's secretary?'

She felt how the annoyance emerged from her insides because the woman couldn't be bothered to remember her name. She mused briefly that it was in Olivia's own interest to be on friendly terms with Ian's secretary, and replied just as bluntly. 'Yes.'

Without any further preliminaries, Olivia explained, 'I've lost an emerald earring over the weekend. I just noticed it was missing. I intended to wear them this evening, and I only have one. We didn't go out when I came down with Ian, so it must be in the house.'

Holly maintained a conciliatory tone and hoped she sounded courteous. 'I only use the office, the kitchen for water, and the toilet when I'm here. If you've lost it in one of the other rooms, I'm afraid I can't help. I can check the bathroom and the kitchen if you like, but I'd prefer not to go anywhere else.' Her colour heightened when she imagined checking through Ian's bedroom where they might have spent some time together over the weekend.

Sounding bad-tempered, Olivia ordered, 'Don't be awkward. I'm only asking you to look for something. Go and check for me.'

Her slight embarrassment faded but her breath still burned in her throat. 'I'm sorry, but I don't intend to pry into Ian's private rooms without his permission. He has a cleaning lady; she's coming tomorrow. If you like, I'll ask her to check. Perhaps Ian could ask his father to look for it. I was just about to finish for the day, but I'll check the guest toilet and the kitchen again before I leave.'

There was a pregnant hush. 'Don't be so pig-headed and foolish.' Olivia laughed softly. 'My dear girl, you must know that you don't stand a chance, do you? Not with someone like Ian. There's no point in antagonizing me. It won't get you anywhere.'

Holly was puzzled. 'What do you mean? What are you talking about?'

With dry amusement in her voice, she replied, 'Oh, come off it. You're infatuated with Ian, aren't you? It was written all over your face that day in the bookshop. You're jealous! How sweet!'

Struggling, Holly could hardly speak. She took a deep breath. 'Don't be silly. You are being ridiculous.'

'Am I? My dear girl, I can recognize hero-worship, adoration and love a mile off. I haven't been on the stage for as long as I have without knowing how to read people's emotions. I can understand why you're attracted — but take a tip from me, and stick to the kind of men you know. Then you won't get hurt.'

Holly was glad Olivia couldn't see her face. 'Ian is my boss. Nothing more, nothing less.'

Olivia laughed nastily. 'Then make sure you don't even think about setting your cap at him. You must realize that Ian is in a class of his own. He'd eat you for breakfast and forget about you ten minutes later.'

Heatedly, Holly retaliated, 'Did you study how to be mean and unpleasant alongside learning how to be a soprano, Miss de Noiret? I suspect that the former skills came easy because they were already deep-rooted in your character.'

Olivia bristled. 'For someone who's paid to shove papers around a desk, you're rude and extremely impertinent.'

'Am I? When someone is being rude, offensive, and making ridiculous assertions, I think I'm entitled to answer similarly.' Trying to calm herself, Holly uttered through thin lips, 'If you want me to search for your earring, get Ian to tell me to. I am paid to run his office. I am not paid to intrude into his private life, unless he asks me to do so. I have no intention of searching anywhere other than in the toilet or the kitchen.

I'm leaving in ten minutes, so it's up to you what you do. Good evening. Phone me back in ten minutes if you want to know if I've found something.' Holly cut the connection.

The woman must be mad. Even taking her artistic temperament into account, her insinuations and resentful attitude were obvious. She wouldn't act so stupidly if she felt confident enough about her relationship with Ian. Silly woman! As if Ian regarded Holly in any other way than his office helper!

She took a quick look around the rooms in question and returned to the office. She tapped a pencil on the edge of the desk, and watched the hands of the clock moving slowly on. After ten minutes, she picked up her bag. Outside, the cool air on her face calmed her thoughts again. She was glad she didn't see Harry, otherwise she'd have been tempted to tell him about Olivia de Noiret's phone call, and to say something that she might regret later.

8

Next afternoon, she'd just arrived and picked up one of the last piles of old information to check, when the phone rang. It was Ian.

'Hello, Holly. How are things?'

'Okay. You too?' She was about to tell him about Olivia's phone call yesterday, when he beat her to it. 'Olivia told me she'd phoned to ask you to search for her earring, and you refused to look for it.'

'I didn't refuse. I told her I wouldn't search your house without your permission. She didn't understand why I didn't want to turn your place upside down on demand.'

He laughed. 'I can imagine. When she gets something in her head, she expects everyone to jump through hoops for her.'

'And she spits poison like a cobra

too.' She heard him chuckle and her heart lightened. Perhaps Olivia imagined he was hers, but she wasn't. If she had been, she wouldn't feel the need to make stupid assertions and hand out warnings to someone like Holly.

'Yes, she's like a prickly hedgehog sometimes. It was Millie's day in the house this morning. Did she find anything?'

Holly shrugged. 'I don't know. I haven't seen her. I never do. I imagine if she has, she'll phone you or give it to your father.'

'I don't mind if you go into the rest of the rooms, Holly. It's polite of you to ask but I trust you. I wouldn't have left you alone in the place if I didn't.'

'There's no reason for me to go anywhere, apart from the rooms I need to use.'

'Well, you know that from this day forth, you can. I'll phone Dad later and find out if he's heard anything from Millie. If not . . . '

Holly decided not to go into details

about the conversation. Her mind still circled Olivia's assertions; she still felt embarrassed and confused by what the singer had said. If Olivia thought she could use Ian to take some kind of revenge, she'd be disappointed. He clearly didn't intend to do anything about it, otherwise he'd have done so straight away.

' . . . Anything else? Any problems?'

'Not really. I sent you a text about Stan Ward and his agreeing to play in Edinburgh.'

'Yes, I've been in touch with him already.' There was a moment of silence. 'And what are you planning this evening?'

'Nothing much. A good book and an early night, I expect. Are you going out?'

'A friend suggested going out for a meal, but I think I'll give it a miss and stay in with a book like you. Now and again, it's good to get away from it all.'

'I bet. David Osborne phoned to tell me he's performing in Swindon on

Friday. I may get myself a ticket and make the effort and go to listen to him.'

There was another pregnant pause. 'You seem to like him.'

'I do: he's unpretentious, and a nice person.'

'Um! Yes, I agree. See you on the weekend, perhaps?'

'Perhaps.'

There was a click. Holly replaced the telephone and stirred uneasily.

She wouldn't see him on the weekend — why should she? She'd never seen him before she started working for him, either.

She went to the concert in Swindon. She borrowed her father's car to get there, and enjoyed the evening. David phoned her beforehand to find out if she was coming or not, and told her to wait for him at the end.

They'd gone to a nearby pub. He was still flushed with his success, and Holly didn't need to pretend when she told him how much she enjoyed his performance. She didn't add that she was thinking about Ian for most of the time he was playing. Holly wondered how Ian felt whenever he attended a performance of one of his performers.

Now, looking across the table at David's lively face and sparkling eyes, Holly could easily imagine another face there instead, and she suddenly realized that Olivia wasn't wrong. She was attracted to Ian. Very attracted. 'Adoration' was going too far, but she admired him and liked him, and she was physically attracted . . .

Holly concentrated on her present partner and told herself not to be so silly. David didn't deserve to be a mere a diversion to stop her thinking about someone else. He was a nice person in his own right.

By the end of the evening, they felt very comfortable with each other. Holly found out more about what he thought about always being on the move, and how difficult it was to earn an adequate living as a professional musician. He was gaining a name for himself, and was confident enough to look forward to the time when he could chose where, and when, he'd play.

He wasn't an egoist. He wanted to know what Holly did, about her hobbies and her family. He sympathized when she told him that ultimately she wanted to have a full-time job and a flat of her own.

He smiled and his blue eyes crinkled at the corners. 'I'm sure you'll get what you want one day.'

Holly smiled back at him. 'And I'm sure you will too.'

They parted. Holly had to drive home, and David to go back to his lodgings. They agreed to meet up again whenever he was performing somewhere within driving distance. He kissed Holly on her cheek, and then softly on her lips, and stood on the pavement to watch her drive off.

Holly saw him in the rear-view mirror, and wondered why someone like him, who showed interest in her, didn't catch her imagination in the same way that Ian did. Perhaps her friendship with David needed more time; that was all. She settled down to concentrate on driving through the darkness. Her thoughts still wandered: most of them centred around Ian — and, inevitably, about how serious his relationship was with Olivia.

★ ★ ★

The following week, Harry mentioned that Ian was in New York. In addition to his business negotiations, he was also planning to attend the premier of Olivia de Noiret's performance in *Carmen* at the Met. Holly tried to show appropriate interest. She had to admit that, as far as appearance and style were concerned, Olivia was the perfect partner for Ian. She was beautiful, famous, and felt at home in the limelight. Holly busied herself with filing the last bits and pieces, and told herself not to dwell on what Ian was doing all the time.

Thursday was stressful in the bookshop. Bill had mislaid a folder they'd prepared for his tax advisors. He'd intended to deliver it on his way home that evening, having promised his advisor the information weeks and weeks ago, and the final date for submission had come and gone. The tax authorities had already issued him with a warning.

Holly had helped him to prepare everything. Now he couldn't find the folder, and his temper and impatience grew by the hour. Holly searched frantically between the haphazard piles of papers and books everywhere in the office. Bill dashed back and forth between the shop and the office, and often messed up and disorganized the piles of things that Holly had already checked. It took all Holly's patience not to get really annoyed and point out that, if Bill had adopted her suggestions about submitting the information on time and clearing up his disarray in the office, it would be a lot easier to find something that had gone astray.

By lunchtime Holly was just looking forward to getting away from it all, and to the peace of Ian's cottage. Bill was in the depths of despair. Gathering her things together, she knocked Bill's briefcase over, and noticed it seemed unusually heavy. Bill normally only used it to transport his sandwiches from home, or as an instrument of symbolic importance when he needed to impress a dealer.

'Bill . . . what about your briefcase?'

Bill's eyes widened and then he hit his forehead with the palm of his hand. 'That's it! Holly, you are a lifesaver. That's where I put it, last night before I went home. Brenda always shoves my sandwiches in there in the morning, so I haven't looked inside it today yet. I forgot all about it.' He grabbed the leather case and loosened the clasp, nodding as he saw the contents. Sheepishly, he added, 'We really ought to get this office into a better shape.

Then we might have had an easier time this morning.'

'I've been telling you that ever since I came here, but you are deaf in both ears.'

He grinned. 'Off you go. I'll see you tomorrow morning.'

Holly left, feeling relieved that the problem had been solved for the moment. Who knew what tomorrow would bring?

She went straight to Ian's. On the way, she met one of Harry's friends in the street. Her smile faded when she saw his expression. 'What's wrong? You look like you've swallowed a lemon.'

'Harry has been taken to hospital.'

She caught her breath. 'Harry? What's happened?'

He shrugged. 'I don't know exactly. Millie found him on the kitchen floor when she arrived this morning, and she called an ambulance. They've taken him to the Royal. I just met Millie's husband on his way home from work. Millie phoned him to tell him what's happened.'

Holly turned and headed for the bus stop again, calling over her shoulder, 'Thanks, Sid. I'll let you know if I find out what's happened.'

Holly's fears grew during the short journey to the hospital. Asking where Harry was in reception, she heard that he was in Intensive Care, but there was no other information. After she found her way to the right department, she was relieved to see Millie sitting in the corridor. At least he hadn't been on his own in the ambulance. She looked pleased to see Holly.

'Hello, Millie. What's happened?'

Millie shook her head. 'The ambulance men said it was most likely that he'd had a heart attack, but no one has confirmed that yet. I've been waiting here for a while now. They won't give me any information because I'm not a close relation. I couldn't give them any details about where to find Ian or how to contact him.'

Holly nodded. 'I'll give them his telephone number. He's not even in the country at present, he's in America.'

Millie looked at her watch. 'I don't want to be unfeeling, but my husband will be home from work, and the kids are due out of school soon too.'

'I understand, Millie. I met Sid, and he told me your husband was on his way home. Thanks for staying so long. I'll try to get in touch with Ian, and I'll tell the medical staff how they can contact him. You go home. As soon as I hear anything, I'll let you know what's happened. Let's hope that it isn't too serious.'

'Being in Intensive Care always means it's serious, love.' She got up and picked up her handbag. 'Phone me as soon as you know something.'

Holly swallowed past a lump in her throat. 'Yes, I will, of course.' Watching Millie hurry off down the corridor, she felt lost for a moment.

Straightening her shoulders, she decided to look for someone who could give her some information. The corridor was empty, and there was a 'No entry' sign on the double doors at the end. Wandering back in the direction she'd come, she spotted an open door and went in. The woman behind the desk was typing, and she looked slightly annoyed when she noticed Holly.

Holly rushed to explain that she needed information about Harry's state of health before she got in touch with his son. A moment later, the woman looked at her in a kinder way, and said, 'I don't think you'll get any information from the medical staff or anyone else, unless you are next of kin. But if his only relative is abroad at the moment, that complicates the whole situation. I'll see if I can persuade one of the doctors to talk to you, but I can't promise if anyone has time, or even if they'll be able to help.'

Holly nodded gratefully. 'I don't want to bother anyone, but I'd like to know what's happened to him so that I can give his son some details, if possible.'

'If you sit in the corridor, I'll try to

get someone to talk to you there.' She reached for the telephone.

Holly complied, glad that at least she had a faint hope that she'd find out how Harry was. It took a while until the swing doors opened and a young doctor came towards her. He ran his hands through his hair and then stuck them in the pockets of his white coat. When he came alongside her, he looked at her with interest.

'Janet explained that you are Harry's friend.'

Holly explained the connection between her and Harry, and why Ian wasn't there.

'I'm sorry, but the rules are very strict. We can't give information about patients to anyone unless they are close relatives, or we have the consent of the patient himself. At the moment, Harry is under sedation, so I can't ask him. Can you contact his son and ask him to get in touch? Come personally, if he can?'

Holly explained. 'I'm sure he would if

it was possible, but he's in New York at present. Can you at least tell me if it is serious or not? I'll contact Ian and tell him what's happened, and I'd like to be able to at least tell him he shouldn't worry, or the alternative — that he ought to come as soon as possible.' She scrabbled in her bag and handed the doctor Ian's business card. 'Those are his telephone numbers, etcetera.'

He nodded. 'If you phone him, tell him to phone us. They'll give you the number in Reception. I can give him the details over the phone, and then it's up to him after that. We're doing our best for Harry. If you'll excuse me, I must get back. The ward is very busy this afternoon.' With a fleeting smile, he turned away.

Holly sat down on one of the hard chairs lining the walls. She felt numb. Picking up the signals from the conversation, she'd decided that the doctor didn't sound too positive. Shaking herself, she scrabbled in her bag for her phone. Calculating the difference in time, it was early morning in New York. The phone rang several times before she heard his voice.

'Hello. Ian Travers.'

'Hello, Ian.'

'Holly?'

'Ian, I'm sorry but I have bad news. Your dad is in hospital. He's in Intensive Care.'

'What!' There was a pause. 'What's happened?'

'I don't know, exactly; no one does. The hospital staff won't give me any information because I'm not related. Millie found him this morning and called an ambulance. The paramedics thought it was a heart attack, but that hasn't been confirmed. The hospital wants you to get in touch, and they'll tell you exactly what's wrong, but they won't tell me — I've already tried without success to find out how critical the situation is. One of the doctors just said he's under sedation. I get the impression things are not too good.'

'I see.' He sounded distant, and there

was alarm in his voice when he asked, 'Do you have the hospital number?'

'No. I'll go and find out, and call you back in a minute or so.'

'Do that, please.' There was a click, and he was gone.

Holly didn't want to bother the woman who'd helped her previously, so she went back to the reception area, and quickly noted the hospital number and the right extension.

She went outside and called him again.

'Ian?'

'Yes.'

'Have you something to note the number?'

'Yes, fire away!'

Holly did. 'When do you expect to fly home?'

'What? What do you mean fly home?'

'Will you be able to get a seat on a plane today?'

'Holly, I am up to my neck in negotiations at this very moment, and Olivia has her premiere this evening.

Perhaps it's nothing serious. I have to talk to the doctors first.'

Holly's breath caught in her throat. 'He is in Intensive Care, Ian. It isn't just a broken arm. They wouldn't keep him there for something like that. Millie found him unconscious on the floor in the kitchen. Do you mean your business is more important than your own father?'

'No, of course not, but . . . '

'But nothing! Then get a seat on the next available flight. If you don't, you may not be able to look at yourself in the mirror tomorrow morning. Do you realize your father may be fighting for his life at this very moment? If you put things off, it may be too late!' Tears were at the back of her eyes. 'For once, put him first before anything else in your life. He deserves at least that much respect and care.' She hit the 'disconnect' button, and stared unseeing at a poster on the nearby wall.

9

After taking a deep breath, Holly decided to return to Intensive Care, in the hope that she would see the young doctor again and that he would tell her more.

She sat, numbly, thinking of how cold-blooded and unfeeling Ian had sounded. Had he always been so rational and detached, or had Juliette and then his business attitude changed him? She went outside to phone her mother and tell her why she wouldn't be home as usual.

Her mother was shocked. 'We were talking to him last night, about the plans for our next flower show. He was fit as a fiddle, and he promised to give Hilda a real run for her money in the competition for the best-tasting tomatoes.'

She went back to the hard chairs in

the corridor again. Nurses and doctors came and went, and after a while the young doctor she'd spoken to previously walked through the swing doors. His expression lightened when he saw she was still there.

He stopped in front of her and gave her a weak smile. 'It's a good thing that you waited. I've talked to Mr Travers' son on the phone. I explained the present state of things, and he told me I was free to pass any information on to you, as he is too far away at the moment to be of any help, and he thinks you'll be a very supportive person for Harry. You are Holly Watson?' She nodded and waited expectantly. 'Harry will be glad of a friendly face, I'm sure.'

'How is he?'

'He had a heart attack. Luckily, someone seems to have found him just after it happened, and we were able to start treatment straight away. There isn't a large section of damage to the heart — but enough, and I'm afraid it's irreversible. His heart will still cope very well, though, and I feel quite optimistic about his recovery. For the next twenty-four hours, he'll be under constant supervision, and once we've done the initial testing and checked everything tomorrow, we can decide on any further treatment from then on. We gave him a light sedative once we'd coped with the immediate dangers, because the hospital atmosphere was making him extremely nervous. He told us he'd never been in hospital before. He's still woozy, but if you'd like to see him for a few minutes you can. His son has already agreed to that, and I think it might help Harry to settle down in the strange surroundings. Would you like to come with me?'

'Yes, of course.' She grabbed her things and followed him.

As they approached the swing doors, he continued to give her information. 'You should only stay a couple of minutes. He needs to relax and get some rest.'

Holly nodded.

'There's no point in you sitting out there in the corridor afterwards either. He is having the best care possible, and if you leave your telephone number with the sister on duty, she'll call if there is the slightest change during the night. You can phone tomorrow morning to find out how he is, and hopefully he'll look forward to another visit tomorrow afternoon.'

The swing doors closed behind her and Holly straightened her shoulders.

It was a brief visit. She could understand why Harry felt nervous and taken aback by the surroundings. The room was full of medical apparatus, and there were continual beeps and signals coming from various machines. Harry's bed was partly curtained off from the others, and he looked frail as he lay there with his eyes closed and wearing a hospital gown.

Holly felt a lump in her throat. She reached out and stroked the hand that was free of any attachments. His eyelids fluttered, and he gave her a faint smile when he recognized her.

'Oh, Harry! I'm sorry!'

'It's alright, love. They are a good bunch of people, and I'm feeling better already. Perhaps if I'd remembered to take my tablets this wouldn't have happened.'

She patted his hand. 'Don't worry about that now. Try to get some sleep.'

'That won't be difficult. I feel really tired. They've given me something to help me sleep.'

His eyelids fluttered and Holly could see it was an effort for him to stay awake. 'I'm going now, Harry. Sleep well. I'll see you tomorrow. You just get better.' She bent and kissed his cheek, before she left him with a final backward glance. His eyes were closed, and he was probably already asleep.

The doctor was already busy with another patient in an adjoining cubicle; he nodded approvingly and gave her a brief smile as she left.

Holly rang the hospital after breakfast next morning and asked to be connected to Intensive Care. Harry had spent a restful night and had eaten his breakfast. She could come for a short visit after lunch. Before she set off for work, she called to tell Millie he was making progress, and they arranged for Millie to pack him a suitcase with his necessities so that Holly could pick it up after work.

When she got to the shop and told him what had happened, Bill was quite shocked.

'I know that the doctor told him to watch his blood pressure, because it was always a bit high . . . but I don't think he had real heart trouble, did he?'

Holly shrugged. 'I'm not sure, but I don't think so. I have the feeling he didn't always take his tablets when he should have. That's always a danger when you live on your own and there's no one else around to remind you now and then.'

'Can he have visitors?'

'Not at the moment. He's still in Intensive Care, but I presume he'll be transferred to a general ward as soon as they feel he's over the worst. Ian gave them permission to let me see him, and I'm going this afternoon. It will still be a short visit.'

'Well, let me know as soon as he can have visitors, and I'll pop in and see him whenever things are quiet around here one morning.'

* * *

Armed with a small suitcase containing Harry's pyjamas, dressing gown, toiletries and slippers, Holly also bought some magazines and chocolate on her way, and was relieved when she arrived in Intensive Care that her friend seemed quite relaxed. He looked up and smiled at her. He was still attached to machines, but he was sitting up.

She smiled back and bent to kiss his cheek. 'Hello Harry! You look much better today. How do you feel?' In their present surroundings, they automatically kept their voices low.

He shrugged. 'Fine. I don't honestly know why I'm in here anymore, I feel fit enough to go home.'

Holly laughed softly. 'I don't think they'll let you do that yet, but I expect they'll move you out of Intensive Care as soon as they think there's no more danger.'

'That's what they told me, too. I notice that you've brought my things? That's great. I feel a right twit in this hospital garb.'

Holly put the suitcase under the bed. 'Tell the nurse when she comes to tidy you up. I'm sure they'll help you get into your own things when they have a moment to spare. I've brought you some magazines and a bit of chocolate. I presume you are not on a diet?'

'Don't think so. I haven't asked. The magazines will be lifesavers. Sitting here with nothing to do and no one to talk to is nerve-wracking.'

'Thought so, but don't overdo it. Have a nap now and then.'

'That's the worst thing about this place. The doctors and nurses are great, but when you don't feel ill, when all the monitors and machines are beeping away, and when someone comes around checking blood pressure or extracting a pint of blood every so often, you can't get to sleep even if you want to.'

She laughed. 'If they took a pint of blood each time, you'd soon collapse. Don't exaggerate, and be patient.'

His eyes twinkled, and a weight fell from her shoulders.

'I'm trying to behave myself, promise. Thanks, love; for coming, and for everything.'

'Don't mention it. Everyone sends their best wishes. My parents, Bill, Millie and her husband, and Sid — and they're only the ones I've met. My Dad rang Sid last night and told him about you being in here, and he'll come to visit you as soon as it's allowed. Can you remember exactly what happened?'

'Not completely. I was on my way to the kitchen to get my breakfast. I felt sick, but thought it was just a stomach upset, or I was hungry and needed something to eat. Then, all of a sudden, I felt one arm go numb, and the pain got worse in my chest. Just before I fainted, it felt like my chest was gripped between the jaws of a vice and someone was tightening the screw. I passed out, and that's something that's never happened to me before.'

'I expect it was very frightening. Luckily, it was Millie's day for cleaning, and she must have found you soon after it all happened.' She tried to sound casual. 'Have you heard anything from Ian?'

'He talked to the doctor after you'd contacted him, and said he'd come as soon as possible. I hope he doesn't drop everything because of me. I feel fine now. There's no need for him to come tearing back.'

Holly didn't comment. She looked around at the other patients. One other man looked fairly normal, and was also sitting up; but he was separated from Harry by two beds, so, even if they'd wanted to talk, they couldn't have without shouting at each other.

They talked for a couple more minutes about general things. Harry asked her to check the garden, and give the flowers and tomato plants in the pots water if they needed it.

'Of course.' She looked at her watch and was surprised that half an hour had passed. 'I'd better not outstay my welcome, Harry. They said I should keep my visit short, but I'll be back tomorrow.'

He smiled and nodded. 'Lovely to see you. Thanks for the magazines. Best wishes to everyone, and I'll look forward to seeing you, if you have time. Don't worry if you can't manage it. I'm being looked after.'

'I'll come, you can bet on it. By then

you'll know if we've forgotten something you'd like to have. Take care. See you tomorrow.'

Holly gathered her things and waved at him once more when she got to the swing door. As she walked along the corridor, she felt relieved that he seemed much better than she expected. She didn't ask to speak to anyone. She didn't need medical details to tell that he was improving.

She'd almost reached the exit when she noticed a familiar tall figure coming through the glass doors. The breath caught in her throat. She was really glad that he'd sorted out his priorities and put Harry at the top of his list. She noticed the worried expression on his face. It was understandable. He didn't know what to expect, and must have come straight from the airport.

He was caught off-guard, and stopped in his stride when he saw her. 'Hello, Holly. I presume that you've been to see him. How is he?'

As their eyes met, she felt a shock run

168

through her. Swallowing the lump in her throat, she managed, 'Much better than I expected. When I saw him last night he looked very frail, but this afternoon — if you didn't know that he'd just had a heart attack, you wouldn't notice anything was amiss. He's still in Intensive Care, and I didn't ask how long they expect to keep him there. Perhaps you can ask one of the doctors?'

His features relaxed a little and his eyes brightened, now he knew Harry wasn't in danger. 'Good. I'll do that.' He paused, and decided that an explanation was expected. 'I came as soon as I could, Holly. You didn't give me a chance to explain. When you phoned, the first shock slowed my reactions, but it didn't last long. I know very well where my loyalties lie.'

She met his glance and nodded. With heightened colour, she said, 'I realize all this isn't any of my business, and I didn't intend to be rude. I just wanted you to realize how serious the situation was. I like Harry very much; he's a nice person. At that moment, I didn't know what had happened, or how serious it was. I only knew he was in Intensive Care, and how I would feel if it was my father. I didn't understand why you hesitated for a moment, or even bothered to mention business commitments.'

He straightened slightly, and stared at her until she looked down to avoid his glance. 'It was only a shock reaction. Common sense kicked in moments later. I didn't have much spare time after I'd talked to you, otherwise I'd have tried to phone back. I booked the next available flight. I had to use the remaining time to reorganize any outstanding meetings.' He ran his hand through his hair. It sprang back into position. 'Some people were annoyed, but most people were understanding. I'm here now. Thanks for all your help. Knowing you had things under control was fantastic, even though I was worried.'

'Millie found him. You can thank her, and the fact that she acted so fast. On any other day, no one would have found him for a while, and it might have been too late. I don't see him every day, even though I'm next door in the office every afternoon. I don't deliberately look for him, and probably no one else would either, unless he's promised to meet someone. When this is all over, you have to pressure him into taking his tablets regularly. I don't think he does, and I don't think he realizes how serious it is if he doesn't. I also think he needs some kind of warning system, like an emergency button. There will always be times when he feels ill. He is getting older, and now his heart is damaged.' Holly didn't want to sound unfriendly or hostile, because she liked him too much, but she knew it was important that he realized Harry needed some kind of extra support. He lived on his own, and had no direct neighbour who might hear if he knocked at the wall in an emergency.

Ian viewed her for a moment. He remained affable but there was a slight hardening of his eyes. 'Yes. I'll see what I can do.'

He didn't like her telling him what he should do, but she couldn't care less. Harry was important, and he had to sort things out before he disappeared again. She met his glance, adjusted her bag, and gave him directions on how to get to Harry. It lessened his fears, and they regained some of their good rapport.

'He'll be delighted to see you. I don't think he reckoned with you coming. He's going to be okay, I'm sure. Bye!'

'Bye, and thanks again.'

Holly had to resist the urge to turn around and watch him. She didn't. She kept her sight on the road ahead and went to the nearest bus stop. On the short journey home, she stared out at the passing countryside, and was mentally free to admit at last that she loved Ian Travers.

Olivia de Noiret was an excellent

judge and a good observer. She had seen the signs long before Holly had herself. Holly wondered why it had happened and when. She only knew she longed for Ian in a way that she'd never experienced before. If he affected her like that and they'd never even touched, how would she feel if they both felt the same?

They weren't more than employer and employee — friends, perhaps — and she didn't always understand him or his motives; but that made no difference. She'd been attracted to him from the start, but had put it down to fascination about someone who worked in a glamorous world. The job was unusual, and he wasn't like any man she'd ever met before. He came from the same background as her, but he now moved in a different sphere, with people who led completely different existences. He seemed to have his life completely under control. He was intelligent and he looked good and attracted her physically. She'd also seen there was a lot of feeling and sensitivity in him, hidden beneath the surface.

Her stomach was knotted as she wondered how to resolve the situation. She didn't fit into his world, never would. It was stupid to remain as an inane little secretary whose insides turned somersaults inside every time she saw him. The rational solution was to find another job. A full-time job, away from the village, so that the chance of seeing him was reduced to a minimum. She'd have to try to hide her feelings till then. She hadn't discovered the truth herself until a few minutes ago, so now she had time to adjust before she saw him again. He didn't come home very often. She'd have time to sort herself out and get used to a life without him.

Holly straightened her shoulders as she noticed her bus stop coming up. It was too late now to go to the office, for the second time in two days. She knew he wouldn't complain about that. She headed homeward, and was glad she could concentrate her thoughts on something else for a while. She didn't need to visit Harry every day as long as Ian was around.

★ ★ ★

Holly mentioned she was looking for a job the next day as she scanned the local newspaper. Her parents had heard her say so before, but her mother looked surprised.

'I thought you liked working for Bill, and for Ian Travers.'

'I do, but they are both part-time jobs, Mum, and I want to have a steady income from one single source so that I can afford my own flat somewhere.'

'I thought you were happy living with us.'

'I am. I'm happy here — and I'm spoiled. I don't have any responsibility. That has to change. All my friends have left home and are independent. It doesn't mean I don't love you, or that I don't appreciate the fact that you're

175

always there for me when I need help or advice. I'm twenty-five, I'm sure I can cope with working full-time, and I need to finance my own life.'

Her father nodded silently. 'If she wants to spread her wings, Kathy, let her fly. I can understand that she wants her own four walls. You and me felt the same when we were young, didn't we? I'll miss not having her here with us if she finds something suitable, but I do understand. I just hope she'll find something not too far away.'

Feeling emotional, Holly looked at him. 'Thanks, Dad. I know I can always count on you both.'

Her mother busied herself at the sink, but a few seconds later asked, 'Found anything suitable?'

Holly shook her head. 'No. I'll look in at the job centre on my way home on Monday. I'd like to find employment somewhere where the company doesn't shut down five minutes after I start there. Somewhere reliable.'

'What about Bill and Ian? Have you told them yet?'

Holly shook her head. 'No, and I don't intend to until I've settled something. I think Bill might even be relieved in some ways. His wife could step into my shoes and do what I'm doing. I've sometimes wondered if he keeps me on out of kindness. Bookshops have a hard time surviving at the moment. Ian will find someone with no trouble. It's an easy job. There's no rush. I can take my time to find something. I stopped looking for a full-time job when I started working for Ian because I was happy with the situation. It's time I shook myself and thought about the future more seriously.'

10

She went to visit Harry again on Monday afternoon. He'd been moved out of Intensive Care, and Ian had organized a private room for the rest of his stay. He looked a lot better. When she arrived, he was sitting in a chair, reading a newspaper. He smiled broadly when she came in.

'Hello, Holly!'

'Hello.' She bent and kissed his cheek and put some fruit on a nearby table.

Gesturing to another chair nearby, he said, 'You shouldn't bring something all the time, it's not necessary. I'm glad to see you. Sit down. Tell me about what's happening in the real world out there.'

'Tell me first about how you are feeling, and what's happening at the moment.'

'As they put it, I'm recuperating. Ian has insisted that, when I'm discharged,

I go to convalesce in Brighton for a couple of weeks. I would rather go home, but he will only worry if I'm on my own, so I've agreed.'

She nodded. 'Super! It will do you good, and you'll be under supervision for the first couple of weeks.'

He laughed. 'You're ganging up on me too, I see. I'm taking new tablets now, too. The doctors say my going to Brighton will mean trained nursing staff can check if something needs adjusting. Generally, people go home from hospital and are referred back to their GP. That's probably just as effective in the long run, but if professionals ensure you are taking the right doses of the right medication from the word go, it's even better.'

'Brighton is a lovely place. I went there on a school outing once. You can go for lots of walks in the salty air. That'll do you no end of good.' She paused. 'Has Ian left for America again, or is he still here?'

'He called to see me this morning

before he left, and is mid-air now, on his way back. He's returning here on Friday to take me to this other place and see that I'm settled in. All the flying backwards and forwards can't be much fun for him, but he insists. He even suggested that I might prefer to go to a well-known health resort in Germany, but I told him that I want to understand what people are saying.' He grinned.

Holly could tell he was feeling a lot better. 'Can I help? Do you need anything special to wear, or take with you?'

'No. Ian has already sorted that out for me. He bought two of these — ' He indicated his smart tracksuit. ' — and will pack the rest of what I need when he comes back. Apparently, I have all I need. He was busy as hell when he was here. He's even organized a panic button for when I come back. Do you know what I mean?'

'Buttons you press when you need help?'

'Yes, quite nifty little things, apparently. You can attach them to your belt, shove them in your pocket, or even hang them round your neck. If you feel woozy, you press the button and are connected to an emergency centre, or someone that you've chosen. They can be programmed to link to whoever you like. I still wonder if I did collapse, and am unconscious, how much use it would be. Ian explained I should press it as soon as I feel anything is wrong. I didn't like to ask him if that included headaches, sore throats or constipation.'

'Oh, go on with you. You know what he means. He's right. That's the whole point of having one. Hanging it on a belt sounds a good idea, but at night something might happen when you're in bed. Around your neck would be better.'

'A lot of fuss, if you ask me.'

'It isn't. You can hide it under your shirt or whatever you're wearing. I bet you won't even notice that it's there after a while. Will you be connected to a professional care centre or someone you know?'

He shrugged. 'We still have to settle that. I'd prefer someone like Millie on the other end, but only if it isn't a bother. Perhaps that isn't fair on her and her family, and an emergency centre would be better.'

'Millie likes you, and her husband is a nice person, too. I hope you'll never need to use it. I can imagine that Millie won't mind, but you can sort that out with Ian's help. I'm sure my mum and dad would be prepared to do it, too.' Holly changed the direction of the conversation. 'How about visitors? Are there any restrictions on the number of people who can come?'

'No, especially now that I've gone private. Ian must have money to burn. I wouldn't have minded a public ward and being with everybody else, but he insisted.'

Holly nodded. 'Good. Several people have asked me, or my parents, if they can visit. Bill will pop in one morning.

When I'm in the shop he can sneak out for an hour. Sid plans to come too, as soon as he knows it's permitted — just like Mum and Dad, and some other people you know.'

'It's very kind of everyone, but I don't expect them to visit me.'

'They know that.'

'What about you? How are you? What have you been doing?'

Holly laughed. 'I'm fine. I haven't been to the office regularly since Millie found you and the ambulance brought you here. I'm going there after this visit, though, because I ought to be earning my money! I checked all your plants yesterday and gave everything water. I'll keep my eye on everything until you come back from the health place, so don't worry about that. If you want something special done in the garden, ask Sid or one of the others to do it, but you don't need to worry that the plants will die of thirst.'

He leaned back and relaxed. 'I'm so glad I live in the village. Just imagine if

I lived in an apartment in the town somewhere. No one would care.'

* * *

Holly busied herself with clearing the last papers, and began to go through the filing cabinet to check that everything was really in the right folder. She wondered where Ian was and what he was doing, but she tried not to dwell on him too much. The more she thought about him, the harder it was to acknowledge that she was planning to leave the office and would never see him after that. It left her with a feeling of emptiness and dismay. She hadn't yet told Harry that she was thinking of leaving, and had decided not to until the moment when she was certain she had another job and everything was settled. She called in briefly to see Harry every day. He had plenty of visitors, so she was content to stay for a short while and leave him to others after that. On Thursday, she wished him well, as she decided not to call on Friday before he left to go to Brighton with Ian. She was still battling with the fact that she had to hide her true feelings whenever she met Ian. She noticed lights in the cottage on Thursday evening when she took Josh for a walk, and she found a note on her desk on Friday afternoon.

Hi Holly,

Just passing through. I expect Harry has told you all about the plans, and I'm taking him to Brighton this morning. I've picked up the list with the telephone calls you've had from people, and I'll get round to answering them as soon as possible.

I'm planning to stay in Brighton with Dad over the weekend, and am flying back to the States on Sunday to tie up some final bits and pieces. Millie knows about the situation and she'll pop in regularly to keep an eye on the cottages. I've been *informed that you are in charge of the watering and Sid has been told to cover diverse other activities. He has us all busy, but I'm really glad he feels well enough to worry about such things again.*

I'll be in touch. Best wishes!

— Ian.

She wasn't sorry to have missed him, because she didn't yet know if she could cope with seeing him. She had to accept that they were ships passing in the night, and was glad she had a little more time to adjust to the idea.

She met Millie when she was on her way home. They hadn't met since the day Harry had been taken to hospital. They chatted for a while.

'Ian brought me a huge bunch of flowers yesterday, to say thanks. He's a nice chap.'

Holly nodded silently. 'He's very grateful that you found Harry and acted so promptly. Who knows how long he would have lain there if you hadn't found him? Too long, perhaps! It's important that a heart attack gets treatment as soon as possible.'

'It was a shock, but I'm glad I found him when I did, too. You've finished work for the day?'

'Yes, off home at last. How's your family?'

'Everyone is fine. My oldest one is going on a school trip next week, so it will be a little quieter around the place.' Millie laughed softly. 'Funny how they often drive you mad when they're around, but you still miss them like hell when they're not there.'

*   *   *

Holly didn't find anything interesting in the newspapers. It looked like it would take some time until she found the kind of job she was looking for. Her best friend Gillian worked for the local vet, and was completely happy with her present job even though she'd previously worked in an estate office. When they met up on Saturday, Holly mentioned she was looking for a full-time job, and was looking forward to the time she'd have her own flat. She didn't mention the real reason: that she wanted to put some distance between Ian and herself.

Gillian nodded. 'I can understand why you want a change. Working for Dr Marsh is a completely different world than when I worked for Fernley's Estate Agency. I earn a little less than I did before, but I feel so much more satisfied. I've learned to handle my money more carefully, and I can still afford everything I need. Dr March and his wife are really nice people, and it's so satisfying to see him help animals. Sometimes he can't provide a miracle cure, but even then he still manages to help their owners accept the inevitable, and that is a gift.'

'That's true! I could look for something out of the ordinary. You did, and it worked out well for you.'

'You've worked in a bookshop, for a

musical director, for a computer firm . . . and when you left school, you even worked for a building firm for a while. That's a lot of very different things. It proves that you can cope with anything. It'd be good for you to have a place of your own. Your parents are lovely, but you need freedom. If you met a boy you really liked, you couldn't even invite him back to your place at the moment, could you?'

'It doesn't bother me. I don't want to rush into a relationship unless I think it is special. I want commitment.'

Gillian shifted. 'Your last boyfriend didn't last long, did he? He wasn't right for you. He was too good-looking, too sure of himself, and had a wandering eye. You should be glad you noticed in time. I've heard he's cheated on other girlfriends since you two split up.'

Holly shoved the hair off her face. 'I am glad. I don't know what I saw in him in the first place when I think about him now. Funny how we seem blind to danger signs until it's too late. Perhaps it's our hormones going haywire. Dad never liked him, and kept telling me so. Mum didn't mind him, but that was probably because he was good at sweet-talking.'

'Ken was very good at pretending about a lot of things. Any new talent on the horizon?'

Holly laughed. 'Talent? It's not easy to get to know anyone properly these days, is it? You know that I don't like discos, and I'm not mad about men who spend their spare time in pubs either. Where do you meet decent chaps these days? Through the Internet, or sport, or clubs of some kind? The only nice man I've met recently is David Osborne.'

'Who's he?'

'Oh, you know, that cellist — the one I went to see him at a concert, and we went out for a drink together afterwards. All quite harmless, but I wouldn't mind meeting him again.'

'Oh, yes, I remember now. He sounds

interesting. Heard anything more from him?'

'Funnily enough, he sent a postcard to say he is playing in a concert in Axminster this weekend, and he hoped I could make it.'

'Well, make an effort and go. Who knows where it might lead?'

'Gill, I am not looking for a boyfriend. I'm happy as I am. David is always on the move because of his work, and I don't fancy traipsing around the country after him.' Holly didn't want to admit it was because of Ian.

'You ought to make an effort to see him; get to know him better. He's based somewhere, even if he travels around. If you like him enough, you could even widen your search for a job to where he is.'

Holly laughed. 'You think I should chase him? I'm not that hard up.' She wanted Ian; she didn't want anyone else. 'Perhaps I should go. Want to come with me?'

'Me? Are you kidding? If it was a James Blunt concert, I'd consider it; but a cellist playing classical music would drive me bonkers. Come on. Drink up. It's my round this time.'

* * *

Monday afternoon found Holly busy with checking the folders in the filing cabinet. Nowadays the office looked very ship-shape, with everything tidied away where it should be. There were a couple of messages on the answering machine, and she'd passed the gist of what those people wanted on to Ian via text. The soft sound of a small portable radio broke the silence and was a soothing companion.

When the phone rang and she heard his voice, she felt intense pleasure, and her heart was in her mouth. It was amazing how he affected her.

'Holly? Thanks for all of the texts. I'll sort them out later.'

She swallowed a lump in her throat.

'Good. How is Harry? Has he settled in?'

'Yes, he seems fine. I phoned just now and he was looking forward to playing dominoes with another chap.'

'That's good. It will help if he has someone else to go for walks and share meals with, and generally pass the time of day.'

'Yes, it seem this other chap is a keen gardener too, and they get on well. It's only for a couple of weeks; but, like you said, it makes his stay much more enjoyable if he can share the time with someone else. How are you?'

'Me, I'm fine. You?'

'Me too. I'm stuck here till the end of the week, but things are working out very well so far, and I won't need to make the trip for a while again, thank goodness. Anything special planned?'

'You mean me? No, not really. I am thinking about going to a concert on Saturday. David Osborne is playing in Axminster. He sent me a postcard to tell me so. It all depends if Dad will lend me his car. If my parents need the car for something, I don't think I'll bother. It's not that far, but I'll have to change train connections, and I don't fancy doing that on my own on a Saturday evening.'

There was a moment's silence. 'Are you and David special friends?'

'You mean, girlfriend-and-boyfriend kind of friends? No. I like him, and he's a nice person, but that's it.'

'Then I'll take you if you like. It will give me a chance to see David in action. I haven't had the chance for quite a while.'

Her heart was pounding too fast. Flustered, Holly couldn't find the right words of refusal straight away. It was tempting, but too dangerous. She liked him too much to spend any leisure time with him. 'Oh!'

'You won't have to drive, I'll do that.'

Grasping at straws in the whirlpool of her mind, she said, 'Will you be back in time? What about visiting Harry?'

'I'll visit Harry too. I'm returning on

Friday. I'll just check the flat in London in case something urgent has turned up there. Then I'll come down on Saturday morning, I might even call to see Dad on the way and take him out to lunch. We can go to David's concert on Saturday evening, and I'll visit Dad again on Sunday on my way back to London. What do you say?'

Disconcerted, she garbled, 'Well, I . . . '

'Good; that's settled, then. I look forward to seeing you on Saturday. I'll pick you up. What time does the concert start?'

Feeling steamrollered, she replied, 'Seven, I think. What about tickets?'

'I'll handle that. They'll hold them for me at the box office.'

'Do you know where we live?'

'Yes, Dad showed me where your parents lived when we were passing on our way home from the pub. Will half-past five be all right with you? That gives us plenty of time to get there without breaking any world records. I know how to get to the concert hall, I've been there several times.'

She nodded to herself. 'I see.'

'Till Saturday, then?'

'Yes, okay! Saturday.' There was a click, and the connection was ended. Holly wondered why she hadn't turned him down. Deep down, she knew why. She wanted to go to the concert with him so she'd have some more memories to keep when she left him. It wasn't sensible, and she'd have to be careful to hide her true feelings, but somehow the prospect and excitement of knowing she was going somewhere with him swept any misgivings and worries aside.

11

She spent a lot of time thinking about what to wear. In the end, she opted for a two-piece outfit in bottle green that suited her colouring and her eyes to perfection. It wasn't new, but she felt good in it; and she reasoned that if she felt good, that was half the battle. She'd seldom been so punctual. If her parents wondered why she was spending time with her boss, they didn't say so.

She felt nervous as she waited for him and tried not to keep looking out of the window. When he arrived, he came up the pathway and knocked. Her mother opened the door and invited him in for a moment, and he accepted. He spoke about generalities and told her parents about Harry. Holly could tell that her mother was impressed. They'd probably seen him around before, but he'd left the village soon

197

after their arrival, and then spent most of his time away in London. The fact that he was wearing a dark suit and a tie was enough to show her he was a young man who knew what was expected of him. Holly just hoped that they weren't picking up the wrong signals. He was her boss, nothing more.

Ian looked at his watch. 'It was nice to meet you, but I think we'd better make a move now, if we are to get there on time.'

Holly's mother nodded. 'Of course. Off you go! Have a nice time.'

Ian smiled at her. 'We will, I'm sure.' He turned to her father. 'I'll see you down the pub when Harry gets back, Mr — '

'Gareth, please. No one in the village calls me 'Mr'. I'll look forward to a pint with you and Harry sometime very soon, I hope.'

On her way out, she thought the whole situation reminded her of when she'd brought her very first boyfriend home for approval. She guessed that her parents were still watching, hidden behind the curtains, and her colour heightened.

Once they were settled in his car, he looked across at her appraisingly. 'Something wrong?'

Still feeling flustered, she was too honest not to say, 'I hope that wasn't too embarrassing. It was like an adolescent introducing her first boy-friend to her parents.'

He laughed. 'No, not at all. Parents are parents. They probably start specu-lating every time someone strange turns up.'

'Yes, but you're my boss. They know that, and should be used to the idea.'

'Holly, I am not embarrassed. Let's go, we can take our time.'

Holly relaxed. They talked about Harry's progress, about the business deals he'd settled in New York, and he told her how he was trying to organize a panic button system for Harry when he got back.

Holly remarked, 'I think that's a great

idea, and it is important. It will give him a better feeling about being on his own most of the time. Is Millie prepared to do it, or are you thinking about an emergency centre?'

'I talked to Millie and her husband, and they seem to be really nice people. I told them that I don't expect them to turn their lives upside down and stop going out, or that sort of thing, but they said they were willing to help. I think he wouldn't like being connected to an anonymous system.'

They joined the motorway and he increased the speed. He was a competent driver, and it was easy to tell he spent a lot of time behind the wheel of his car. 'If Millie isn't home, they'll send a team out to check on him. It took a little persuasion, but he saw sense in the end!'

Holly laughed softly. 'That sounds okay. What do the doctors say? Is there a lot of permanent damage?'

'Enough. He'll need to take medication from now on. As long as he does that and goes for regular check-ups, there is no reason he shouldn't live to a ripe old age.'

'Good. He admitted once that he did occasionally forget to take his tablets. I persuaded him to buy a container with the days and times already marked out, so that he can see at a glance if he's taken things when he should have. But I'm not sure how effective that will be.'

'He wouldn't admit it, but I'm sure this whole business has given him a fright, and I think that it will make him more careful about taking medication when he should.' Ian ran his fingers through his hair briefly. 'That aspect bothers me, too. It makes me wish I was around a lot more than I am. I intend to cut back on travelling, and try to spend more time at home with him whenever possible. I'd like to be able to keep an eye on the situation personally, and not have to leave it up to other people all the time. He is my responsibility.'

'Don't tell him that you feel responsible for him, he'll have another heart attack. He'll tell you he's a grown man and you don't need to worry about him.'

'I know, but I'll try to change things as unobtrusively as possible. He already knows I intend to restrict the number of new clients, so when I start reducing other aspects, I hope he won't get suspicious. I honestly have been considering cutting back on the travelling for a while now. I don't think he'll connect that with anything to do with him, unless I go about it in a completely ridiculous way.'

'That would be very good for him. Just for him to know you are planning to be home more often will go a long way to make him feel better. Perhaps you ought to get a check-up yourself. Sometimes heart trouble is hereditary.'

He nodded without commenting, and indicated to exit the motorway. The country roads were quieter, and Holly relaxed. She didn't want to ask him about Olivia's premiere in the Met, but it came up in the conversation anyway. It seemed that it had been a resounding success. He added, 'I wasn't there, I was on my way back across the Atlantic; but I saw a performance the following week, and she was really impressive in the role.'

'I can imagine. She looks like Carmen, doesn't she, and she has a wonderful voice.'

He guided the car to an empty space on the side of the road and they joined a stream of other people heading to the concert hall. He left her for a moment to pick up their tickets. Holly wondered if she should offer to pay for hers, but decided not to mention it. It was likely that he hadn't paid for his own either. On his way back to where he'd left her standing, someone from the organization stopped him. They spoke for a minute or so until Ian nodded in her direction, shook the other man's hand, and hurried to her side.

They had excellent seats and the

acoustics were really good. There were several artists and David played a piece by Brahms. It was haunting, and she thought yet again how he was someone with a lot of talent. When he took his final bow, his eyes swept across the audience; and when he found her, he gave her a special smile. Holy was very aware of sitting next to Ian all evening, and sometimes they touched as they shared the programme or resettled in the seats. Her heart thumped erratically and a shiver of wanting ran through her. He looked at her sometimes and gave her a knowing smile that made her heart skip a beat. The evening couldn't have been better.

When the concert ended, after several curtain calls the room began to empty and they made their way out. They waited for David in the vestibule.

When he arrived, Holly smiled and said with enthusiastic honesty, 'You were so good, David. I was lost in the music. I expect every cellist plays the same piece of music in a slightly different way, but the way you played this evening was quite unique.'

David shoved a stray lock back from his forehead. 'I'm so glad you enjoyed it.' He looked at Ian. 'I'm surprised to see you, Ian.'

Ian looked knowingly. 'It was a spur-of-the-moment decision, and I don't regret it. You were very good. Excellent, in fact.'

David looked pleased, and then glanced across at Holly. 'I'd hoped we could share a meal together . . . ?'

Ian answered, 'Good idea. Why don't you get your cello, and then we'll go to a little place not far from here. I booked a table earlier this evening.'

Holly was surprised, and at first David looked a little disappointed that they were going to be a trio, but he hid it well.

* * *

The restaurant was renowned for its food, and they discovered it had earned its reputation. The dining room had a warm and welcoming atmosphere. There were three floor-length windows that dominated one wall. They overlooked a wide stone terrace dotted with evergreens in large terracotta pots.

Holly soon noticed that Ian kept hogging the conversation. Every time David tried talking about something Ian couldn't relate to, Ian started expounding on something completely different. David was too polite to ignore the interruptions, so he sometimes stopped in midstream and listened to Ian instead of finishing his own tale. Holly mused that Ian was his agent, and no doubt that was a strong argument why David didn't antagonize him by butting in on his conversation. Holly still couldn't figure out what was going on. It wasn't how Ian usually behaved. He was generally reserved and listened more than he talked. That wasn't the case tonight.

When Ian was busy ordering them wine, she looked at David, tilted her head, and lifted her eyebrows quizzically. David clearly understood what she was trying to say, and shrugged discreetly. Ian drank sparingly himself, only finishing one glass, but encouraged the other two to enjoy more wine with the meal. She twirled the stem of her glass, and listened while the two men talked about David's next performances and Ian mentioned the name of someone he'd engaged to accompany him.

David was naturally more interested in that kind of information at the moment than in his friendship with Holly. Holly knew that he liked her, she could tell, but this evening Ian wasn't giving them a chance to get to know each other better or to let the discussion include much personal detail.

By the time they ordered an espresso, Holly almost wished she'd never told Ian she was coming to see David again this evening. At the same time, she knew she was lying to herself: she loved being with Ian. It was something to remember. Her confusion, longings, and thoughts of coping with a future without Ian whizzed around her brain. She'd revelled in the journey here and looked forward with being alone with him on the return trip. This evening was special. When she finally left Ian's office, she'd have to find other things to make her life worthwhile in other ways, but she didn't want to think about that tonight.

She hoped that she'd keep in contact with David. Perhaps he wasn't looking for a serious relationship . . . but then, she already knew she couldn't offer him more than friendship. Maybe they'd meet again — or not: that was all in the future.

Holly was almost relieved when the meal ended. Leaving a couple of notes on the crisply starched white table-cloth, Ian got up, and David and Holly joined him. They reclaimed their coats, and it took a little longer for David, because the waiter had to fetch his cello from an adjacent room.

Reunited outside, they all stood together for a moment. David held out his hand to Ian. 'Thanks for the meal, Ian, and thanks for coming to the concert.'

Ian smiled. 'You're welcome. Keep up the good work. People are beginning to notice you at last. I've had a couple of enquiries about possible performances in the USA. I'm hoping to arrange a couple of evenings with Manfred Ostman accompanying you. I have the feeling it might give you just that extra push that sends you straight to the top.'

David's eyes sparkled. Holly guessed that her presence wasn't what he'd most remember about this evening. Hearing that Ian was busy planning his future career prospects was. His voice mirrored his excitement. 'Really? That would be super!'

'I'll be in touch.'

Looking like a little boy who'd just found a longed-for Christmas present under the tree, David remembered his manners. He turned to Holly. 'It was lovely to see you again.'

'That goes for me too! I'll keep my eye out for when you're performing somewhere within travelling distance. Although, when you get really famous, I might not be able to afford the tickets!'

'You can depend on the fact that if I ever top the bill, I'll send you a free ticket every time.' He leaned forward and kissed her cheek. 'Take care.'

'You too.'

Ian lifted his hand in farewell and began to walk away. Holly followed him with one last backward glance at David. He was positioning his unwieldy cello case in the most sensible position for him to carry. His shadowy figure strode off jauntily in the opposite direction, clearly still busy with thoughts about possible forthcoming appearances in America.

When they reached Ian's car, he waited until she was seated before closing the door. Holly noticed how even the slightest touch had the power to stir her. The moonlight fell slanting on his cheek as they drove from the town. The streets were dark and narrow at first. Holly glanced out of the window and willed herself not to constantly look in his direction. Scudding clouds hid the moon now and then. The road bent and zigzagged on their way back to the motorway. There was soft music playing on the radio. Holly felt obliged to say something.

'I enjoyed the evening. David played really well, didn't he? I'm no great judge of classical music, but when he was playing I found myself lost in the sound.'

'And what did you feel?'

'Melancholy, sadness; and towards the end, there was a spark of optimism again.'

'Not bad judgement, considering that your music interest doesn't centre solely on classical music. Some people go to the bother of reading up on what a composer thought when he was writing a particular piece of music, but I think everyone should follow their own instincts when they're listening. Next time when you hear exactly the same piece of music, you might be in an entirely different mood yourself, and end up with a completely different feeling about it.'

They reached the motorway and he joined the evening traffic smoothly. It wasn't too busy, and this part of the journey was less interesting because the scenery was shadowed and the road was straight.

Holly wondered if she should mention she was thinking of looking for another job; it was a good chance at this moment, and he wouldn't be able to study her face much. She stared ahead into the darkness, and decided she'd wait until Harry came back from his convalescence, and until she knew his panic button was functioning. By then, she should be feeling strong enough to face him; she wasn't at present.

She came back to reality when she

heard Ian ask, 'Do you want a coffee, or anything else? There's a service station up ahead.'

'No, thanks. I'm fine. Don't let me stop you having something if you like.'

'No, I don't fancy anything either. We'll go straight home.'

'When are you leaving tomorrow?'

'Early. I'm calling to see Dad before I drive on to London.'

'That's a lot of driving in one weekend. Do you ever think about accidents?'

He laughed. 'I enjoy driving. You do get some strange thoughts, don't you? You have to leave it up to fate. You can't avoid your destiny.' He overtook another car and pulled into the inside lane again. 'You could step off the pavement in the village and get knocked down by a drunk driver.'

'Um, I know that, but the chance of an accident increases with the amount of time you spend driving.'

He glanced across briefly through the shadows. 'I don't think about it; I never have. If you start worrying about 'what if', you may as well lock your door and throw the key away. I don't take unnecessary chances, I try to drive sensibly, and I stop if I feel the slightest sign of fatigue. Motorway driving is usually extremely boring, and I make regular stops every couple of hours if it's a long journey. Satisfied?'

Holly nodded in the darkness. 'It sounds okay, but I still think the possibility increases, even if you drive properly. It's just common sense.'

He took his one hand off the steering wheel for a moment to reach out and ruffle her hair. 'What would I do without you worrying about me and my father?'

'Whatever you did before, I'm sure!'

They had left the motorway, and were soon in familiar territory. When they reached the village, it was already too cold for anyone to be outside; the streets were silent. She noticed a man who lived on the other side of the village out walking his dog, and someone else who was winding his way home from the pub.

Ian drew up outside her parents' cottage. Light was shining through the gap in the curtains in the downstairs living room. Her parents were still watching television. Holly released the seatbelt and half-turned to him, barely seeing his face properly in the darkness.

'Thanks for taking me there, and bringing me back. Give my love to Harry when you see him tomorrow.'

'I will.'

She was too surprised to react when his hands slipped up her arms, bringing her closer. She stared at him, tongue-tied, and their eyes met in the darkness. For a moment time seemed to stand still, before he leaned forward, kissed her gently. The kiss deepened and sent waves of delight through her as he recaptured her again. This time it was more demanding, and emotion upon emotion exploded so fast she couldn't keep up. Her senses reeled as if she'd been short-circuited. He released her, and she wondered why he'd done it and if he'd explain. Perhaps it was just a routine thing for him once he knew a girl well enough? She hoped there was more to it than a mere meaningless task that he thought she was expecting after he'd invited her out. She took an audible breath.

His voice sounded slightly gruff. 'I shouldn't have done that, should I? After all, I am your employer.'

Trying to gather her scattered wits, she tried to sound nonchalant. 'It does muddle things a bit, but just briefly. I don't think that it makes too much difference, does it? Not really.'

He shifted. 'No, I suppose not. The temptation was too great.'

If Holly expected some other kind of explanation, she was disappointed. She fumbled to open the door and he leaned across, reminding her just how much she wanted to be held close to that strong body. He pulled the right lever and the door opened. Holly swung her trembling legs out onto the pavement and stood up. When she turned to close the door, she smiled weakly though the dividing window, rippled her fingers in farewell, and then turned towards the house. She covered the short distance without looking back, and heard the car moving away.

She scrambled through the contents of her bag looking for the key. She was still a bundle of excited nerves. Before she opened the door, she stood for a moment, leaning against the framework and frozen in time. She touched her lips with her fingers. She had to steady her thoughts and appear as if nothing important had just happened. Her parents would expect her to at least pop her head around the door to tell them whether she'd enjoyed the evening or not. She had to ignore the fact that something she'd longed for, for days, had just happened. She hoped her expression wouldn't give her away when she told them that she'd had a wonderful evening. Only then could she escape to her bedroom under the eaves and think about Ian and his kisses.

She lay awake for a long time wondering about what had happened, and felt no wiser about why he'd done it when she finally fell asleep.

12

They were unusually busy in the shop next morning, so she could concentrate on something else for a while. It was different when she got to Ian's cottage. It was so silent and the fact that she knew there was no one in Harry's cottage next door only heightened the sense of isolation. The only sound she heard was the ticking of the grandfather clock in the hallway downstairs. She busied herself with routine things, but she was still distracted as she thought about him. She wandered to the window. The trees outside in the lane were heavy with leaves and the sky was blue. The sound of the telephone brought her back to earth in earnest. Her heart accelerated when she wondered if she was about to hear Ian's voice.

'Ian Travers' office, Holly speaking.

Can I help you?'

Holly's anticipation crumbled when she heard Olivia. 'I still haven't found that earring. Have you looked?'

'Hello, Miss de Noiret! No, I haven't found it; but as I haven't looked for it, that's not surprising, is it? I think I told you last time you asked me about it that I never go into Ian's rooms. He told me he'd talked to you and explained. He has since given me permission to go anywhere in the cottage, but I prefer not to. Did you get in touch with his cleaning lady?'

Her voice was snippy. 'I haven't got time to go running after domestics. I asked Ian to ask her. He did, and apparently she hadn't found anything, so I suppose I have to believe her.'

'Well, if she hasn't found it, I can't suggest anything new.'

Olivia's voice was subtly suggestive when she said, 'It was a present, and I'm sure that it cost a lot of money. Emeralds of that size and quality are quite special. I can easily imagine that anyone would be tempted to keep it and sell it, if they found it.' She was silent for a moment. 'It would be a bit of a risk, of course, because even if it is redesigned and used in another piece of jewellery, I might recognize it. I intend to keep my eyes open, and if I ever find it again, the person who stole it will be very sorry.'

For a moment, Holly continued to listen without feeling concern or disquiet, but then she wondered if Olivia was hinting that she thought Holly or Millie was involved in some way. 'I hope you're not suggesting that Millie or I would do something like that?'

Olivia laughed softly and paused for a moment. 'No, I don't think you would be stupid enough; but you never know what people will do when they're desperate for money, do you?'

Feeling her hackles rising, Holly refuted, 'I assure you, I have not seen your earring. I don't even know what it looks like. I suggest you check through your own possessions again before you begin to suggest someone else has done something unlawful.'

'I've looked.'

Feeling her anger was ready to boil over, Holly retorted, 'Well, look again! Millie is as honest as the day is long, so don't dare suggest she is involved; and hardly anyone else apart from her or me comes to Ian's house. Perhaps you lost it in the garden, or in the car. Perhaps it's still in your handbag, or in your suitcase. Perhaps you are just making wild accusations for reasons only you can understand. If you'll excuse me now, I have to get back to my work.'

With the receiver still in her hand, she heard Olivia's faint voice: 'Well, really. Why Ian puts up with someone like you, I can't imagine!'

Holly sat for a moment, feeling furious with the stupid woman. It looked like she was determined to blacken Holly's name for some reason, but accusing someone of theft was going too far and it had to stop. She couldn't contact Ian at present; he was abroad, and she could hardly send him a text stating 'Your girlfriend is going gaga!'.

She yanked one of the drawers of the filing cabinet and took out a bundle of folders. She forced herself to concentrate, and even managed to notice some documents that had been stored in the wrong places. Holly missed having Harry to break the hours between coming and leaving. Their chats were always about things she understood. She found it hard to understand how Ian could put up with people like Olivia, and hoped that when he thought about marriage he would choose someone a lot nicer. She even managed to forget about last Saturday for a minute or two because her anger about the contents of her conversation with Olivia was still raging inside. She had to begin the slow and difficult job of working out what do without Ian in her life.

Holly now wished she'd asked Ian for Harry's telephone number. She didn't have his temporary Brighton address, either, otherwise she might have asked to borrow Dad's car on Sunday and gone to visit him.

The rest of the week passed and she heard nothing from Ian. That wasn't unusual, but time seemed to drag. She looked at prospective employment in the local newspaper; there wasn't anything that caught her imagination.

Ian phoned on Thursday, just as she was about to leave. Her pulse increased and she felt flustered.

'Good, Holly, I've caught you. I wondered if you'd already left. I just got in from the airport. Everything okay? I rang Dad yesterday, and he's fine.'

Holly decided not to beat about the bush. 'No, everything is not all right! I wish you'd tell your girlfriend not to keep phoning me to ask about her blasted earring. She called again Monday about it.'

'Did she? She doesn't usually worry about things like losing jewellery, and Olivia is not my girlfriend. She's just a client and a friend.'

'I told her last time she rang that I do not intend to invade your private rooms. I also told her to ask Millie and your father. This time it sounded like she thought Millie or I had filched her blasted earring and sold it on the black market.'

'Oh, come on! She didn't accuse you of stealing it, did she?'

'Not in words, but the insinuation was there, and I don't like it. I don't like being accused of pinching other people's property. I don't want to pester you with our bickering because I know you've been busy with other things, but now that you are back, I'd be grateful if you tell her not to bother me about it again.'

'I don't understand it. When it comes down to the bare facts, it's her own fault she lost it. Trying to needle other people won't bring it back, so why should she bother you all the time?'

'For the same reason as before! She doesn't like anyone who gets close to you in any way. She's possessive.'

'Nonsense! What do you mean, 'the same reason as before'?'

Holly hadn't intended to blurt that out. 'Oh, never mind about that. Just tell her to get off my back, will you? If she phones again casting false aspersions, I'm likely to lose my temper, and then she'll be on to you again, telling you to get rid of your bad-mannered secretary.'

His voice was measured. 'I wouldn't get rid of you no matter who said what.' He paused. 'Leave it with me. I'll have a word with her and I'll get back to you, promise. Get off home now. It's already past your working time. You'll be charging me overtime if you hang around much longer.'

There was a click and the connection was cut.

13

She didn't expect to see him over the weekend. She hadn't asked about his trip to Norway, but presumed it had gone well. Saturday evening, she met Gillian. They went to a pizzeria and then on to a pub for a chinwag. Gillian was in the throes of a romance with someone she'd met by chance. Holly felt slightly jealous when she listened to Gillian gushing about her new boyfriend. It sounded like this time Gillian had found herself someone she'd dreamed about at last. Holly was glad that she didn't need to contribute much to the conversation. She could sit back and listen to her with half an ear. She had never gone into any explanation about what she felt about Ian, because there wasn't anything special to tell. Gill just knew he was Holly's boss, did interesting work, and mixed with rich and famous people. Holly hadn't added that she'd fallen head over heels in love with him. She knew her friend would tell her to be careful, and warn her it might be a kind of star adulation that would eventually dwindle and die.

On Sunday afternoon after lunch, her dad was settled comfortably in his slippers with the newspaper, and looking forward to the sports show on TV. Their dog had other things on his mind. Josh sat in front of him with his head on the side, trying to stare him out. Holly could only smile at his efforts to attract attention, and felt sorry for him.

'Come on, Josh, I'll take you.'

Josh didn't need to be asked twice. He shifted his attention to her. His backside and tail waved excitedly in expectation.

It was a fine afternoon. She set off with a delighted animal. Her fleece jacket and denims were just right for walking the lonely woods and fields near her home. She reached one of her favourite spots, let Josh off the lead to explore on his own for a while, and thrust her hands in her pockets. Making herself comfortable on the crossbar of a stile leading into a field, she watched him running around in frantic circles. There were some ancient oak trees with gnarled and thick trunks on the fringe of the nearby wood. The green leaves of the trees were waving in the light wind, and fugitive breezes skimmed across the grass, finally reaching her to briefly play with her hair. Sunlight was fighting its way through the passing clouds and most of the time it managed to win the battle. It was a perfect afternoon for a walk.

She reminded herself to check the local paper when she got back; perhaps there would be something suitable on offer this weekend. She needed an alternative, something to keep her busy, when she left Ian. Finding a flat and decorating it might help fill the immediate gap too. Once Harry was back and safe in his cottage again, she'd keep in touch with him, but move on to a job that didn't bring her into contact all the time with the one man in the whole of her life that she yearned for. The fact that she'd most likely never see Ian afterwards lay like a heavy rock in her heart already. She tried to tell herself that when she moved from the village, not seeing him would make things easier and might help cure the ache.

She'd keep in touch with Harry as long as she could avoid meeting Ian. She and Harry had always bumped into each other long before she started working for his son; especially when she was out walking with Josh. Ian didn't come to the village most weekends, so she could still call in to see Harry on the off-chance. She watched the diminutive white dog racing around after something that was indiscernible from this distance, probably an insect. It was nothing short of a miracle that he hadn't been stung before now. His pink tongue was already hanging out as he panted his way after his unsuspecting quarry. Holly smiled at his antics and efforts to catch something that was faster and more agile than he was himself. She jumped down, brushed the seat of her pants, and called Josh. His head shot up and he looked in her direction, but it took a couple more calls from Holly before he reluctantly raced towards her, his short legs thrashing the grass as he came. She bent to attach his lead. He was panting heavily.

'It's your own fault if you're thirsty. Come on, we'll go as far as the brook, you can have a drink, and then we'll go home.'

'Can I come too?'

The sound of his voice sent shivers down her spine. She swivelled round. Her heart thundered in her ears and she hoped he couldn't hear it. 'Ian! What are you doing here?' She stuttered slightly. 'I didn't expect you to come down this weekend.'

Standing on the other side of the

stile, he looked very comfortable and relaxed in fawn linen trousers and a casual sweater with the collar of a check shirt peeping out. The wind ruffled his hair and Holly had an urge to reach out and touch him.

He replied smoothly, with no particular expression on his face, 'I visited Dad, and decided to call on the way back to London.'

With a lump in her throat she said, 'That's a big detour, isn't it? How was he? Was there a special reason you had to come? Something to do with the office?'

'Not with the office — something else I wanted to clear up. I just heard you tempting Josh with an extension to his walk. I'll come with you, and tell you why on the way.' He looked up at the clouds racing far above them. 'I saw you sitting on the stile and parked the car just around the bend.' With tongue in cheek, he added, 'You looked like a little leprechaun sitting there.'

She laughed. 'I think leprechauns are

wizened old men, aren't they? Do I look like a wizened old man?'

One corner of his mouth turned upwards. 'No, far from it. You are more like Titania.'

'I'm not sure that's an improvement. She may have been Queen of the Fairies, but she fell in love with a donkey.'

He laughed and bent to ruffle Josh's head. 'Hello, old chap! Right — ' He looked at her. 'Shall we go?' He offered her his arm, and Holly had little choice. She tucked her hand in the bend of his elbow, and they set off.

She tried to hold on to normality. It was unreal and exciting to be with him at this moment. 'Do you know the brook?'

He indicated with his chin. 'Of course. It's just ten minutes away, into the wood. I used to spend a lot of time there with friends. It was a perfect spot for harmless adventures like building dams and other games. We often played football in this field.'

Holly liked the idea of him playing here as a kid. 'Oh, of course. I forget that you lived here long before we came to the village.' They made their way up the gradual slope of the field that smelt of wild flowers and fresh grass until they reached the first fringe of trees.

'Why don't you let Josh off the lead? Or will he run away?'

'No. We come here often, it's one of his favourite spots.' She set him free and Josh shot off into the undergrowth. Ian held out the palm of his hand. She gave in, although she knew the danger of doing so, when she placed her hand in his. Their fingers intertwined and the feeling made her flesh prickle. It was a sensation she'd never experienced so strongly before. She felt comfortable with him, but also sexy.

They walked on wordlessly for a time. There was a well-worn pathway through the thick bunches of trees and shrubs, and sunshine leaked smidgens of gold through the greenery here and there. They soon heard the sound of the brook. Nothing else except the chirping of birds broke the silence as they went soft-footed towards its banks. The surroundings were blanketed in a shimmer of green that gave the place a magical feeling. Clear water flowed over moss-covered rocks and smooth pebbles, and the stream hugged the stalks of ferns and other water-loving plants growing haphazardly along its embankments. They stopped when they reached a nook at the edge of the water.

Trying to think of something sensible to say while trying to control the lump in her throat and her racing heartbeats, Holly commentated, 'This would be a perfect background for Titania in *A Midsummer Night's Dream*, wouldn't it?'

He looked at her, ignoring their surroundings, and nodded. 'Perfect!'

It was hard to remain coherent when they were this close. She wondered how she could possibly live without seeing him in the future. She forced herself to say something sensible. Her voice was still unsteady when she asked, 'How's Harry?' She took the chance to free her hand and pushed the hair out of her face.

'I already mentioned that he's fine.'

She nodded, and her senses reeled as she looked at his face. Knowing that she loved him made her legs turn to jelly.

'I think he understands now that it's imperative that he remembers to take his medication on time. They're also giving him talks about healthy eating and things like that. He's struck up a friendship with someone else who is there, so on the whole I'm sure he's making the best of it and enjoying the stay, although he's also itching to come home.' He continued to study her. 'He asks about you constantly — and the others in the village, of course.'

She had rarely had so much time to study Ian unhurriedly. She viewed him, feature by feature, and despite the whirl of emotion knowing she would have to leave him, she also knew he was all she'd ever wanted. Swallowing the lump in her throat, she commented, 'Good. I'm glad. How much longer will he stay there?'

'Another two or three weeks.'

She nodded and looked around for Josh. He was busy digging a hole.

'I talked to Olivia about her phoning you.'

Her voice sounded calm again. 'Did you? I hope she now realizes there's no point in asking me the same question continually? Check through the cottage again, and tell her you've done so.'

'I already did that last time I was home. I don't understand why she keeps bothering you about it.'

She cleared her throat. 'Ah, well! Who understands the rich and famous?'

'Something you said made me think you do understand her motives and why she's so persistent. Do you? As I know you are one of the most honest people I've ever met, I'm sure you have no problem telling me the why and wherefores.'

Awkwardly, she cleared her throat. 'I don't want to cause unnecessary friction by being bitchy about her. I just got mad. You're used to her. I'm not, and therefore I'm prone to overreacting. It doesn't really matter what she said or why. If you've told her she should be more careful in future, that should suffice.'

Flatly, he said, 'I'd like to know exactly what she said that upset you.'

Her colour heightened and she gave up pussyfooting around. He clearly wanted to hear the truth. 'The first time she called about the earring, she claimed I was being unpleasant because I was infatuated with you and I should back off. The last time, she made hidden suggestions that Millie or I could have stolen it, and that was the straw that broke the camel's back.'

There was a glint of satisfaction in his eyes. 'I thought it might be something like that. Why didn't you just tell me what she'd said at the time?'

The silence of the wood surrounded them and threatened to stifle her breathing. Half in anticipation, half in dread, she answered, 'It embarrassed me, and I thought it might embarrass you to hear she thought I was in love with you. I didn't want us to feel uncomfortable with each other.' Her face was aflame. 'That would have complicated things. I've thought a lot about what happened and what she said since then. Perhaps a change isn't such a bad idea. A new secretary would be a new beginning, and I ought to be looking for a full-time job.'

His eyes widened. 'A new beginning? A full-time job? What do you mean?'

Holly couldn't tell him the whole truth. She shrugged and ploughed on. 'Olivia is an important client, and we don't get on. My obvious negative reaction to her is wrong, and I can't hide it. It's not a professional attitude and could cause you problems.'

'Holly, you never embarrass me, and

you are professional. Your honesty is stimulating, and nothing Olivia or anyone else says can come between us. If someone is rude, you have the right to retaliate. I appreciate how you run the office. I was delighted to see you sitting on the stile just now — it meant I didn't need to find an excuse to get you alone somewhere else. I came wholly and exclusively to see you.'

She played desperately with the lead in her hand. 'What for? You just said you haven't come on business.'

There was now something lazily seductive in his look, and he shook his head. 'No, it has nothing to do with business.'

She grew hot and cold and her stomach tightened. The very air seemed electrified and his nearness made her senses spin. She waited and he reached out for her hands again. His thumbs fondled them, and Holly felt a warm glow growing inside.

His expression was serious. 'I hope that what Olivia suspected is the truth, because I'm having immense difficulty in concentrating on business these days. I find myself thinking about you all the time.'

'Me?' The breath caught in her throat and her voice croaked.

He smiled his wonderful smile. 'You're surprised? I thought how I felt about you was pretty obvious. Especially after acting like a first-class idiot during our trip to David's concert. I tried to grab the conversation because I didn't want to give David a chance to impress you. I wanted you. I've been wondering how to get from being your employer to being the man in your life for a long time, but I didn't know if I had a chance. The evening of David's concert, I still didn't know how to handle the situation. I couldn't resist kissing you. Afterwards, I wondered if I'd scared you off, because I was so panicky I let you get out without explaining properly. I lost a perfect chance to find out what you felt for me.'

Holly stared at him, confused.

'When you told me about Olivia needling you, it started me thinking. You're not easily annoyed if someone else is rude or insensitive. Olivia is not someone who cares about lost jewellery. I wondered if there was some mutual enmity going on between you, and as I was the only link that might be causing friction, it gave me hope.'

As casually as she could, she uttered, 'Olivia wants you and she doesn't want any competition.'

'And — are you competition? Do you feel more for me as a person than as your employer?'

Holly decided there was no point in avoiding or pretending. Her mouth and lips felt dry. 'Yes, my feelings have spiralled out of control . . . but I didn't want you to be embarrassed. I've decided to move on. I've already started looking for a new job.'

He pulled her into his arms. His breath warmed her face and she saw desire in his expression. 'Dear God, stop even contemplating that, this minute. Never leave me! I love you. I never thought it would ever happen again after the disaster I experienced with Juliette, but gradually I fell in love with you more and more every time we were together. I love everything about you.'

Holly's lips opened slightly in surprise, and he had the perfect chance to kiss her. His mouth covered hers hungrily. She was powerless to resist; not that she wanted to, anyway: this was what she'd been longing for. His nearness kindled feelings of fire. Raising his head, he gazed into her eyes, and she saw what she hoped to see.

It was impossible to steady her erratic pulse and her voice sounded stunned. 'I can't believe this is happening.' She tried to be sensible. 'But I don't fit into your world! I'm too countrified, too unsophisticated . . . ' He silenced her with another kiss and wrapped his arms around her to draw her so close that they stood as one.

He said, so softly it made her heart

ache with love for him, 'Don't talk rubbish! Just tell me you love me as much as I love you. Put me out of my misery.'

She nodded. 'Of course I do.'

He threw back his head and shouted, 'Wow! And I've been worrying for weeks. I've worried and wondered how you felt about me.'

She tried to hang onto sanity and be sensible. 'I am not the kind of woman you need alongside you, Ian.'

'Don't be stupid, my love! You're everything I need. Don't be deceived by my lifestyle. You know by now that it isn't always glamour and glitter. My work is important to me, but I've also discovered that other things in my life are more important. You are. You give my life a reason. If you were mine, I'd have something money can't buy. At first I just liked you, but then I realized I was falling more in love with you every time we were together. You are honest and caring and beautiful, and I love you.'

She tried to throttle the bubble of sheer happiness growing inside. It was impossible. 'You're sure?'

He nodded. 'Absolutely. Definitely. Unconditionally. Undeniably!'

Holly's smile mirrored her delight when she realized he did love her as much as she loved him. 'I can't believe it.' Awkwardly, she cleared her throat. 'I hope you realize I don't want an affair. That's not me. If you're just planning me as another fill-in, another temporary girlfriend, please stop now.'

He laughed softly. 'I haven't been serious about a woman since Juliette. I'm quite sure now that I didn't love her, not really. I didn't want to fall in love, and I never expected to. I stopped believing in love . . . but you have changed all that. I want to grow old with you. One day I want us to have a family. I want a life of commitment, but commitment that has nothing to do with business. I want you, Holly Watson.'

She was powerless to resist him when

he looked at her like that. She replied, with some of her returning complacent buoyancy: 'That's good, because that's what I want, too. I don't know how I'll cope with us being apart so much, but I'll learn to handle it. You have to take the bad with the good when you love someone.'

He appraised her lazily, and laughed softly. 'I have no intention of us being apart more than necessary. I want you with me. I want you with me wherever I go, whenever it is possible. We'll keep the cottage, of course, and alternate between here and London like I did before, as long as it's sensible to do so. I do intend to cut back on all the travelling, but whenever I can't avoid it, I want you with me. You'll get a chance to see various places while I'm busy, and now and then we'll share some of the surroundings together. Sometime in the near future, I can imagine stepping down; and either employing someone I trust to take over long-distance problems, or changing my direction completely and concentrating exclusively on events in the UK. When we have children, I'd like to be around to see them grow up.'

With heightened colour, she replied, 'You've got it all worked out, haven't you?'

'I hope so, but I'm open to other suggestions — your suggestions — and I'm guessing that you want the same things.'

She nodded silently, and her eyes sparkled.

His smile contained a sensuous flame. 'Let's go back to the cottage and open a bottle of champagne to celebrate. Harry will jump over the moon when I tell him. He mentions you constantly, which always gives me a wonderful chance to talk about you. I think he already knows something could be on the boil. I hope that your mum and dad will be glad when we tell them too?'

'Probably, but it'll be a bit of a shock, because they assume you are nothing more than a good employer.' Tongue in cheek, she added: 'That's a thought — are you doing all this just to get your office work done for nothing?'

His eyebrows lifted and he threw back his head and let out a peal of laughter. 'I hadn't thought about that aspect, but you have a point there.'

'What about Olivia?'

'What about her? I don't know why you are so bothered about Olivia.'

'Because of the way she acts, things she hints at, as if there's some kind of special relationship between the two of you.'

'We went out as a twosome a couple of times, a long time ago, but I never felt anything special for her. As soon as I realized she was looking for more, I tried to make her understand that; but she didn't want to accept it, even though I deliberately tried to avoid private rendezvous from then on. She forced those weekends on me by pretending she needed to get away from the pressure of rehearsals in London, claiming that her artistic achievements would be lessened if she didn't.'

She slipped her fingers under the collar of his jacket and pulled his face closer towards her own. 'She was hoping for more than a casual relationship.'

His eyes were twinkling. 'Perhaps, but even though I kept telling her I definitely wasn't interested, she tried twisting my arm for professional reasons. I really thought she was worried about her performances, and that I could calm the situation by allowing her to come to the cottage. The first time she came, she probably intended to impress me with her compatibility, and she was on her best behaviour for most of the time, but I've known her too long. She's a very demanding personality. I can't begin to understand why she thought love was going to suddenly blossom when it hadn't happened earlier. After a relatively short stay, she stormed off in a huff when she noticed I wasn't coming to heel so it wouldn't be the romantic tête-à-tête she wanted. The second time, when she kept pushing for another invitation, she said her nerves were at breaking point. I didn't want to be the agent who did nothing to help . . . She hoped I would change my mind, but I didn't. I was already under your spell the first time Olivia came and ruined my weekend. By the second time, I knew just how much I wanted you. No one else stood a chance, or ever will in the future.' He paused. 'We did not share the same bedroom either time, in case you're wondering about that.'

She laughed. 'I did wonder, actually; but I believe you if you say so. Come here!' She pulled him close and kissed him in a way that told Ian that things were going to work out just fine.

'Will she now drop you as her agent?'

He shrugged. 'Who knows? I don't care. If she hopes to get a better deal elsewhere, she's welcome to try. I've seen her rise to fame, and her tantrums have grown with her.' He was motionless for a moment as he studied her face. 'You are worth a million Olivia de Noirets. You are incomparable.'

They were beginning to feel sure of each other, and shared the delight; free to show each other just how much they cared. After a while, they made their way hand-in-hand back through the field. Glancing at each other, arms entwined, stopping for a kiss and parting more reluctantly every time, they strolled back to his car and drove to the cottage for some iced champagne. There they could relax and talk about their future together with increasing euphoria.

Sitting next to Ian, Holly sank into his shoulder with a sigh of pleasure. He wrapped one arm around her and pulled her closer, handing her a long-stemmed crystal glass with the other. They both revelled in the knowledge that they now belonged to each other.

'Here's to us!'

Holly clinked her glass and leaned forward to kiss him soundly before she took a sip of champagne. 'To us!'

We do hope that you have enjoyed reading this large print book.

Did you know that all of our titles are available for purchase?

We publish a wide range of high quality large print books including:
Romances, Mysteries, Classics
General Fiction
Non Fiction and Westerns

Special interest titles available in large print are:
The Little Oxford Dictionary
Music Book, Song Book
Hymn Book, Service Book

Also available from us courtesy of Oxford University Press:
Young Readers' Dictionary
(large print edition)
Young Readers' Thesaurus
(large print edition)

For further information or a free brochure, please contact us at:
Ulverscroft Large Print Books Ltd.,
The Green, Bradgate Road, Anstey,
Leicester, LE7 7FU, England.
Tel: (00 44) **0116 236 4325**
Fax: (00 44) **0116 234 0205**

Other titles in the
Linford Romance Library:

INTRIGUE IN ROME

Phyllis Mallett

Gail Bennett's working holiday in Rome takes an unexpectedly sinister turn as soon as she arrives at her hotel. Why does the receptionist give out her personal details to someone on the phone? Who is the mysterious man she spies checking her car over? Soon she meets Paul, a handsome Englishman keen to romance her — but he is not what he seems. And how does Donato — Italian, charming — fit into the picture? Gail knows that one of them can save her, while the other could be the death of her . . .

THE FAMILY AT CLOCKMAKERS COTTAGE

June Davies

Feeling bereft after her sister Fanny gets married and moves away, young Amy Macfarlene must manage Clockmakers Cottage on her own, while earning a living as a parlour maid and seamstress for a wealthy local family, the Paslews. Her wayward brother Rory is a constant concern, as he is clearly embroiled in some shady dealings and refuses all offers of help. Amy's childhood sweetheart Dan is a comfort to her — but as her friendship with the handsome Gilbert Paslew grows, so do her uncertainties about her future . . .

RACHEL'S FLOWERS

Christina Green

Rachel Swann takes a sabbatical from her London floristry job to come home and temporarily manage the family plant nursery. But then it emerges that her uncle has also asked the globetrotting plant collector Benjamin Hunter to do the self-same task! Wary of Ben's exotic plans for the establishment, Rachel is determined to keep the nursery running in its traditional manner. But as the two work together, they cannot ignore the seeds of a special relationship slowly blooming between them . . .

UNEASY ALLIANCE

Wendy Kremer

Joanne is intelligent, capable — and beautiful. Her female colleagues always assume this plays a major part in her rapid promotions, no matter where she works, and now all she has to show for her efforts is her current state of unemployment and a string of short-lived jobs on her CV. Signing up with an exclusive dating agency, she meets tycoon Benedict North — an exceptional, charismatic man. But when she finally lands a job, Joanne is unsure of whether there is room in her life for him — despite her growing feelings . . .

WEDDING BELLS

Dawn Bridge

Marina is attending her widowed father's wedding when she is immediately drawn to handsome fellow guest Roberto. A romance soon sparks between them, but it's anything but smooth sailing ahead when Marina discovers her old flame, Jon, has lost his memory, and visits him in hospital. Torn between trying to help him and spending time with her new love, Marina is distraught. Can she and Roberto overcome their difficulties and find happiness together?